The Isle of

Book (

of

The Assiduous Quest of Tobias Hopkins

by

James Faro

Cover Illustration:
Market Day in Dominica by Agostino Brunias

CONTENTS

Chapter 1 – Survivors

As if the raids on the town of Maracaibo were not enough to witness, the blameless crew of the Maryland brig were also forced to endure the loss of their ship. After two long weeks the bloodshed and looting of innocent towns had finally ceased and most of the flotilla had now headed out to sea.

It was misfortune that *The Chesapeake Venture* was one of the last vessels to leave the Spanish colony for, by the time she reached the bar, the tide was already beginning to run. Despite a steady breeze calling from the ocean beyond, the vessel had had enough. Like a stubborn dog she buried her keel into the sand and refused to move.

For the Spanish fort at the western point of the channel the opportunity was too good to let go and the brigantine became a steady target from that moment on. Already scarred from a week of battering, there was little hope for the vessel. It was decided that all hands should abandon ship; not such an easy task as the French who had commandeered the vessel had already slipped away in the cutter an hour before. The remainder of the crew were now at the mercy of the sea. As luck would have it, an English barque had anchored on the windward side of the sandbank to pick up the survivors.

With one fist clamped to a forestay the last man aboard stretched his body full length over the bowsprit of the vessel and tried to grab the base of the sail which was now flapping defiantly over the starboard bow. If he could just bring it in there was a good chance he could save his vessel and fate will change. He could then take the brig downwind and slip her over the sand bar before it was too late.

Having spent most of the morning lifting men from the wreck strewn waters, the crew of the English vessel had expected the task to be over by now and were waiting to weigh anchor and head out to sea. All eyes were fixed on the stranded brigantine one hundred yards off the port bow.

Lieutenant Hackett, Captain of the vessel, stepped up to the gunwale. "Is that the last of them?"

One of the seamen nodded towards the brigantine. "One more to go, Cap'n."

Hackett frowned at a figure perched on the bowsprit of the abandoned brig.

All eyes were diverted to the shore as a distant boom sounded from the Spanish fort. Seconds later the iron went crashing into the sea less than twenty feet off the stern of the stranded vessel; yet this last man didn't appear to be in a hurry to leave.

At a distance his appearance seemed hardly that of a merchant seaman. Not only did he appear to be younger than most of the survivors they had taken aboard, but his clean shaven features, boyish face and fashioned hair were more akin to a city-dweller than that of a seaman. The crew looked to one another as a second shot fired out from the fort. This time the ball ripped through the rigging of the vessel. And yet, unconcerned, the stoic figure seemed only interested in reaching for something over the bowsprit of his vessel.

Tobias Hopkins, the man at the centre of the crew's attention, wiped the brine from his eyes and set his mind to the task at hand. The forward jib, the only sail intact, was playing a game of catch me if you can, flapping in the breeze with its sheet trailing out over the starboard bow. If only Toby could find something that would reach – a pole, a staff, anything long enough to bring the rope aboard.

Another distant crack and Toby looked across to the fort to catch an angry trail of white smoke drifting out into the bay. He ducked behind a cable housing as a whistling sound, gentle at first, approached from the shore. Within seconds the sound increased to a screaming crescendo as it passed somewhere over the mizzen yard. The ball hit the water with a crash about twenty yards off to starboard.

Toby returned to his task. He searched amongst the wreckage littered across the forecastle deck – nothing there. The main deck was worse – broken spars, tangled ropes, ripped canvas everywhere. The vessel had taken on serious list and most of the wreckage was heaped up against the port gunwale. Toby surveyed the pile. His eye caught something; a glittering metallic light calling to him from the shadows. He took a closer look. Buried deep beneath the splintered wood was a band – a gold band which was attached to the finger of a very pale arm. Who the arm belonged to he had no idea. All the surviving members of the crew had been mustered before abandoning ship, so who was this? He reached forward and gripped the man's wrist. With feet placed apart he gave one mighty heave. The next moment he was on his back; hands still clinging on to the wrist. The wrist was certainly attached to an arm, but that was all: no body, just an arm, pale and torn with a bone protruding from a matted tangle of veins and sinews.

Then he remembered. This was Nathaniel Lathan's arm. The unfortunate man had been stationed on deck when the main mast came down. The vessel took on such a shake that Nathaniel fell to the deck and landed his right hand into a coil of wire. The mast came crashing to the deck and the wire shot up to the sky taking the man's arm clean away from his body as if it were a twig from a dry bush. Toby looked at the limb. Not much use to Lathan now, he thought. However, he may be pleased to have his ring returned. Toby tried to ease the band off the finger, but it wouldn't shift. He took his knife from his belt, sliced through the digit at the knuckle and pocketed the ring.

He had been wondering what he should do with the Nathan's arm. Should he just toss it over the side? He looked over to the waiting English vessel and, for the first time, noticed the crowd of onlookers gathered at the gunwale. Embarrassed by the notion, he let the appendage slip from his grasp and drop to the deck hoping his watchers weren't able to read his thoughts. His eyes dropped to the breaking surface of the frenzied waters on the windward side of the bar which was now tinted with the colour of death and wondered how many of his crew had made it to safety. Another shot came from the fort across the bay, this time sending a tower of spray a few yards off the stern. Toby stuffed the arm back amongst the wreckage in the hope that any neglectful thought would be buried with it. He got to his feet. There may be something he could use below.

The silence was strange below – unexpected, somewhat eerie. Normally there would be much activity on this deck but, without the presence of crew the silence was unworldly. The scent of burnt powder still hung in the air as if the shots had been fired only moments before. The gangway along the main hold was in much the same condition as the decks above. A number of canons had escaped their moorings and blocked the gangway as if to say they had had enough. Powder kegs were overturned with their contents strewn over the planks. Canon irons, like French boules, were about the deck everywhere. Toby's eyes wandered to the bulkhead of his handsome brigantine where the French sea-robbers, in their crude manner, had hacked through the hull to make six gun ports. And what use had they been? Most of the canons had been salvaged from Spanish galleons and didn't fire at all, and those that did were about as accurate as Cromwell's musket.

Another crack from the shore reminded Toby to get a move on. Lying across the port side of the hatch was a ramrod, a pole of about five feet in length – just what he was looking for. He took one step forward then stopped. Slumped against the base of the mast housing was Owen Fuller. While the nature of this poor man's demise had been reported to him earlier that day, Toby was not prepared for the sight which was presented to him now. The man was well turned out; a clean singlet and dusted breeches, even his shoes looked as if they had been respectfully polished for the occasion. In fact, Fuller was as well turned out as he was the day he enlisted aboard *The Chesapeake Venture* three months before. Healthy in every respect except for one – his head was missing.

Fuller would have been facing the starboard bulkhead when the incident happened. Toby looked over his shoulder. At eye level, a clean round opening of about six inches diameter had been pierced through the hull of the ship. The ball, which passed with equal force through the port side of the ship, would have taken Fuller's head off in an instant. There would be little point in looking for it now.

He dragged the body over to the canvas awnings stacked in the corner and heaved the man onto the pile. He wrapped the top sheet around the body and fastened it with a length of lanyard. Once done, he lifted Fuller over his shoulder and dropped him onto the deck at the nearest gun port. Toby considered the package for a moment, then left, returning a minute later with the Holy Bible in his hand. Turning to Psalm 107 he started to read aloud.

"They that go down to the sea in ships, that do business in great waters, these see the works of the LORD, and his wonders in the deep. . ."

When he reached verse twenty-eight there was a resounding crash and the whole brig shook like a baby's rattle. There was no crack of canon fire, nor a whistle to warn him, just a deafening crash as the ball. Like an iron fist, splintered its way through the port side of his ship.

He raised his voice. "He maketh the storm a calm, so that the waves thereof are still."

Then came another sound: a rushing sound of water entering the bilge space below his feet.

It was now only a matter of time.

"Then are they glad because they be quiet so he bringeth them unto their desired haven."

With that, Toby snapped the Holy Book closed and lifted the body to the gun port. It was as Fuller was suspended half way through the opening that Toby had a thought. The last thing he wished to do was give the sharks a free offering in the way of a body bag. He rested Fuller's feet on the deck and fed a cannonball into the lower part of the canvas tube. Once secured, he pushed the body through the port. Toby stuck his head through the opening. For a few moments the bag floated on the surface of the sea then, with a final dying breath, sank to the depths below.

The ship gave a sudden lurch followed by an unhealthy creaking as the stern began to rise above the waterline. Toby raced to the upper deck, returned his Bible to his kitbag and crammed the remaining space with as many pieces of splintered wood as he could lay his hands on. Without a second thought, he leapt over the starboard rail and allowed the current to take him over the bar towards his rescuers.

As soon as the word went out that the man had gone over the side the crew of the Lady Charlotte once more gathered at the rail of their vessel. The tide was running fast now. With his kitbag supporting his head, the man slipped over the bar and raced towards them, his lifeless body lying face-up amidst a trail of blooded water. At that point the crew took him to be finished.

But Tobias Hopkins was far from being dead. Rather than make a commotion in the water and attract the attention of hungry sharks, he chose to lie perfectly still, his thoughts occupied with the arduous task ahead. As he was lifted from the infested waters, his main concern was, not for himself, but for the well-being of the crew of his vessel. And particularly the well-being of John Fowler, for without him his next task would be impossible.

He was somewhat disappointed at his welcoming as he was dragged over the rail. He perused the crowd who had gathered around the gunwale to meet him. The disorderly group appeared to be no different than the company of French buccaneers he and his crew had been forced to endure over the past few weeks. Their clothing was conventional enough – canvas or linen knee-length slops, waistcoats and plain linen shirts – most had adorned themselves with an accessory of sorts. For some it was an earring of gold, for others a shark's tooth or some other sort of trophy. And all were armed with a general disregard to safety; pistols tucked into cummerbunds and muskets propped against the gunwale. There was a sense that these men had little regard for authority, for most of the company were either leaning against a bulkhead or remained slouched on the hatch cover.

Soaked and bedraggled, Toby's first words were to enquire of the whereabouts of his Mate. With no response, he straightened up, slung his kitbag over his shoulder and surveyed the bemused onlookers. "Would one you good gentlemen be kind enough to direct me to Mister Fowler," he repeated.

A man dressed in a naval lieutenant's jerkin stepped forward from the crowd. "And who, may I ask, are you?"

Toby frowned. "Hopkins. Tobias Hopkins, Master of the Chesapeake Venture."

This statement was greeted with a few chuckles from the group.

The naval man held up his hand. "Give the boy a chance." He turned back to Toby. "But we were told that the vessel was commanded by a Monsieur Lafaiette."

"The vessel was commandeered from us when we were set on course for Barbados. They held us hostage and took us on to Tortuga. The Chesapeake is a merchant vessel…" Toby looked up toward the empty horizon, "was a merchant –"

"That's as we thought, Captain Hopkins. Those French butchers couldn't handle a canoe let alone a brigantine. You will be pleased to know we set them adrift in a cutter to let the Spanish deal with them."

A member of the group, who had been running a kerchief through the barrel of his pistol, leaned across to his shipmates. "Ha! An' pissin' their breeches, they was too."

The man in the naval jerkin leaned with his back against the gunwale. "I am Captain-Lieutenant Hackett and I am in command of this vessel. Welcome aboard the Lady Charlotte, Captain Hopkins." He nodded toward the stern. "You will find your crew over there on the poop deck."

Toby thanked him and was about to take his leave when one of the group looked up from his game of dice and raised his hand. "You forgettin' something Captain? Or should I say 'Master'?"

Laughter erupted from the crowd.

The Lieutenant addressed his crew. "Leave him be. I have my doubts the boy could stay afloat for long with his pockets laden with takings." He turned back to Toby. "You are welcome aboard, Mister Hopkins. We are now bound for Port Royal on the Island of Jamaica. Have you been there afore?"

"No, I fear I have not, Lieutenant."

"Then you *are* in for a treat."

The crowd roared.

Since mid-morning the survivors of *The Chesapeake Venture* had been mustered on the poop deck where John Fowler, a bear of a man with wavy light-brown hair and a beard which hid much of his genial face was calling out names from the vessel's crew list.

"Henry Jackson?"

"Aye." A man standing in the front of the gathering raised his hand.

"Matthew Wilkins?"

Silence.

"Matthew? Where's Matthew?" There was a note of panic in the Mate's voice.

A young hand of about fifteen years pushed to the front. "Here I am, Mister Fowler."

John let out a sigh of relief. "That's fine, lad. Just stand easy." He placed a mark against the boy's name. "You all together, Son? Not been hurt, have you?"

"No, Sir."

"Good." John gave a concerned glance over to the abandoned mizzen deck where the crew of the Lady Charlotte had been gathered at the port rail. He returned to his list.

"Taponket? Samuel?"

"Aye." The gentle reply came from the back; a seaman who stood a good head and shoulders above the rest. Samuel, a Yaocomico Indian who could lift a top spar with one hand, had been *The Chesapeake's* bosun from the very beginning.

The Mate was about to call the next name when there was a distraction amongst the crew. He looked over his shoulder to see his captain making his way up to join them. Toby moved to the poop rail while the men who had followed him from the main deck sat around to watch the proceedings.

John, somewhat relieved, continued with the roll.

"Simon Croft?"

The name was greeted with an empty silence. All looked to their captain as the name was called again. The look on the crew's ashen faces was to haunt Toby over the next weeks.

"Went down with the starboard skiff, Chief."

All eyes turned to Jackson.

"His feet was tangled in the rigging when she went down. Sucked under like a lead, he was."

A man squatting on the hatch, removed his pipe and stabbed the air. "If those French bastards hadn't overloaded that skiff with canon irons he'd be here with us now!"

This evoked a response from the crew; "Aye, aye!" "True enough." "Butchering bastards!"

"Alright now. Let's get on, shall we?" John Fowler read out the next name.

"Davies?"

The man with the pipe blew out a cloud of smoke. "John, you know I'm here. I was just talking with –"

"Yes, bear with me. Let's get this job done properly, then we can move on." Fowler marked Davies as present.

Toby, who had been standing aside during the proceedings, felt that a degree of formality was required. "May I intervene for a moment, Mister Fowler?" With his speech prepared, he stepped forward and addressed his crew. "Gentlemen, the raids along the coast are now over and God has spared us."

These opening words elicited a few looks amongst the privateers who had followed Toby from the mizzen deck.

"No longer do we have to endure another day with the scent of blood on our hands," Toby continued. "We should now put all this behind us and set to –"

"Forgive me, Captain." Fowler moved close to Toby and gave a nod towards the gathering of onlookers. "With respect, but now may not be the right time to say too much on that topic, do you not think?"

Toby frowned at their audience who, in turn, waited for a further response from *The Master*.

"As you wish, Mister Fowler, but I would like a private word with you when you've done."

"Aye Captain," John nodded. "May I also suggest that you get that arm seen to?"

A pool of fresh blood was dripping onto the deck beneath the captain's right arm. "Point taken, Mister Fowler, I'll do that right away. Carry on."

Toby left the company and was directed to the purser's quarters where he was bandaged, given a hammock and an issue of rum. Armed with these items he took claim of a quiet corner on the forecastle where he laid out the contents of his kitbag to dry.

Chapter 2 – **The Word of Jack Bride**

It was mid-afternoon when John Fowler caught up with his captain. The Mate glanced at the items on the hatch cover – a flintlock pistol, a knife, the Holy Bible, a small writing case, some papers held together with cord, a singlet and a pair of cotton breeches. He frowned at the neat pile of splintered wood. "They thought you were for Davy Jones' Locker before they heaved you aboard."

"I didn't want to attract the attention of sharks."

"Aye, I guess."

"So now, how many do we have?" asked Toby.

The Mate looked up, confused.

"Hands, Mister Fowler. How many hands have survived this day?"

"Oh, I fear we have only eleven, Captain." Fowler checked his list. "Isaac Jacobs, Henry Jackson, Matthew Wilkins –"

"Oh yes, young Matthew. His maladies returned this morning so I understand. How does he fare now?"

"Fully recovered it seems, Captain."

"Good, good. Best we keep an eye on him though." Toby paused in thought. "Who else is still with us?"

"Samuel Taponket, Robert Davies, Daniel Fish, Michael Strowd, Marcus Dodds, Michael Talbert, Nathaniel Lathan, although he was badly injured yesterday."

"Who was?"

"Nathaniel, Sir. I fear he may lose more than his right arm."

"Oh yes, I found it for him this morning." Toby buried his hand deep into the pocket of his jerkin.

"You found his arm, Sir?" John Fowler followed the captain's movements with a look of incredulity.

"No, no. Well yes, I did discover his arm as it happen. However, the item I was referring to is this." Toby pulled out the gold ring and handed it to John. "Would you be so good and pass this on to Mister Lathan?"

"Of course, Sir"

"Has he reported to the purser?"

"He's there right now."

"Well let's pray he will come through. Is there anyone else?"

"One more. Joseph Freeman."

"And of the casualties?"

"Of those lost today, Owen Fuller met with a canon ball as we sailed past the town's defences. Adam Milward was in the storeroom when that French grenade went off, and John Bucher, Simon Croft and Richard Hobson didn't make it to this vessel."

Toby moved over to the rail. "So, that's five lost today, adding to the four over the past two weeks. It's a terrible thing, John. A terrible thing."

"Aye, that it is Captain."

Toby tried to focus on the deep blue water beyond the wake of the vessel as she headed out into the Caribbean Sea. The Spanish Main was all but a thin dull line which severed the horizon like cut from a vicious blade. His vision of the *Chesapeake Venture*, swallowed by a running tide, was all but a distant memory. All that remained was an aching vision of those of his crew who were lost. This was their worst day yet. Of the original twenty-two men enlisted when *The Chesapeake* set out from Saint Mary two months before, only thirteen now remained. This was not even their war. Nor was it his crew's choice to embark on bloodied raids against Indians and innocent Spanish settlers. These were God-fearing men whose only mission was to elicit a peaceful trade along the seaboard to the north.

Toby straightened up and moved away from the rail. "Well, we should count our blessings. The Lord has saved us once again to live another day."

"Yes. But, with respect Captain, the crew of this vessel may have had something to do with that, do you not think?"

"Quite so, quite so. But what of our casualties. How are we going to tell their families, John? Do you know their families?"

The Mate frowned.

"Oh, yes, yes of course you do." Toby was distracted with the task at hand. If he were to regain any kind of respect from his remaining men, he would need to find, in the briefest of time, a way of returning them to their homes. Now, without a vessel, the task would seem to be insurmountable.

"How much money can we muster?" he said.

"Money? I really don't think –"

"If we are to return these men to their homes."

"The dead?"

"No, the survivors. We will need to purchase a new vessel. Did any of the crew manage to salvage anything from *The Chesapeake*?"

"Well, yes and no. What I mean is, the French loaded up the cutter with as much of the bounty as they could lay their hands on. So there was no chance anyone from our crew could pocket their share and hope to swim to safety."

"So, that's the no, Mister Fowler. And the yes?"

"It so happen' as soon as the French tried to come aboard this vessel, the crew confiscated the lot and sent them adrift in the cutter."

"So this vessel has now made a claim on it?"

"Not quite. Lieutenant Hackett will honour our share providing we allow them a commission for saving our souls."

"What kind of commission?"

"Sixty-forty in their favour."

Both men were silent for a few minutes.

"What choice do we have? They could run us all down at a word."

"That be so, Captain."

"Just to think," Toby shook his head. "If those French swine hadn't taken us on this misadventure we'd be in Barbados now, loaded up a profitable cargo of sugar and ready to sail back home. All the crew would be alive and well."

"There is some talk of that place of late."

"What talk?"

"There has been, in the last month or so, some rebellious mischief among negro slaves of that Island." John Fowler looked for a response from his Captain. "At leased that is what the crew of this vessel are saying."

"Exaggerated, no doubt."

"It's said that a revolt was planned to take place this month. And they say that if the plan hadn't been discovered the slaves could have easily taken over the island as locusts in a cornfield."

"Surely the authorities will take control of these people."

"With respect, Captain, I ain't so sure of that. The slaves number more than twenty to each white man."

"What is the fate of these perpetrators?"

"Thirty-five of them are to be executed." John paused. "But some have escaped the Island."

"What do you make of this story, John?"

"If this crew are to believed, I'd say it's a blessing we didn't venture there."

"Maybe, but under what circumstance?"

John Fowler looked over to a small group of Chesapeake survivors collected on the mizzen deck. "Aye Captain. That be so."

That evening there was much merriment and rejoicing amongst the crew of the Lady Charlotte – claims of heroism, appraisals of bravery, excited they were as hounds returning from the hunt. It was obvious the raids were a success. So why did Tobias Hopkins choose not to share this victorious moment with them? At least the ordeal of the past few weeks was over – no more the taste of cannon powder, the fear in men's eyes, the looting of Maracaibo! So what harm could there be if, just for once, he was to take that one step closer to his fellow men and share rejoice in their victory? Toby shifted uneasily in his hammock. He was tempted. For what was the alternative? Soon the night would slip him away, take him to a place far worse than the camaraderie on deck.

If there was any truth in the tale John had related, then the voyage to Barbados and the search for Toby's father would need to be postponed to a later date. Not the he had any choice, now that he had no means of getting there. Misfortune it may have been to watch his own vessel go down, but had it not been for the English barque, both he and his crew would certainly have gone down with it. Or even worse, had the *Lady Charlotte* not been waiting for them, the Spanish would surely have picked them off.

And now, with the winds from the south and a clear night sky, the barque was out in the open sea bound for the Island of Jamaica – wasn't that good enough reason to celebrate? He stared into the blue-black sky, determined to keep the veil of sleep from him, wishing that, just for once, his recurring night-dream would leave him in peace.

Toby breathed in the cool salt air and looked up to the stars – so big he imagined he could touch them. He reached up to the night sky and immediately the pain began to throb. He sat up. Legs astride of the hammock, he loosened the linen cloth from his right arm. All he could see under the moonlight was a long black gash running from his shoulder to his elbow, impossible to tell if the wound had healed. He took the flask from his jerkin and squeezed his eyes tight. Like a touch from a smiths white-hot iron, a searing pain shot up his arm as he poured the spirit along the wound: in a perverse way, a welcome change from the eternal throbbing he had been forced to endure throughout the day. He wound the cloth back and fastened the knot with his teeth. Toby could now look forward to the return of the familiar pulsing throb.

He took in a deep breath of salty air. Now they were a few leagues from the coast a steady breeze had picked up. He rested back and took in the sounds around him; the whistling in the rigging, the unceasing tapping of the stays against the masthead and the slapping of waves against the hull as the vessel made its way northwards. These familiar sounds were occasionally broken by the voices of the crew. Toby listened to their brave words.

After all the atrocities of the past week there was no mention of cowardice, no declaration of fear, for these words were not to be spoken amongst hardened men. How could he bring himself to be part of the camaraderie shared between these raiders? These same men who, on that very day, he and his crew had witness slaughter over sixty folk of a defenceless town? How could they not feel the same repulsion as he? The voices around him became more distant, the words more obscure. Toby was drifting.

He quickly sat up. Sleep had almost taken him.

Exhausted, he rolled out of the hammock and made his way to the mizzen deck. There, amidst a gathering of hands, were three of his own men. On seeing their captain they called him over to join them.

A seaman from the crew of the *Lady Charlotte*, looked up. "Hopkins, is it? Twice I sailed from Jamaica with a man of that name."

"A common enough name," Toby replied.

"Aye, sure enough."

The man, a hardened privateer of about fifty years of age, shrugged and turned back to his comrades. Toby now recognised him as one of the crew who had fished him out of the water that morning. On first meeting, the man gave the impression that he could be a tempestuous fellow, one to whom it would be best to give a wide berth. But here, surrounded by an audience of heedful shipmates beneath the southern stars, this sea-rover was as excited as a child.

"Twas when I were sailing under Captain Morgan." The old salt eyed the group seated around him. "A hard one to beat if there ever was. Never knowed one to match him, not afore, nor since.

Morgan were liken to the Devil himself. And cunning as a fox too, I seen it with my own eyes." The man paused to take a swig from his ration. "We sailed right into Portabello, just like it were Bristol town. A flotilla of over a dozen ships and five hundred men we were, and the Spanish didn't have no clue we was coming."

Toby had heard this story many times back in Tortuga, each a different account to the last. However, this privateer, whom none would doubt had run his cutlass through a score or more, was probably more experienced than many who claimed to have sailed with the notorious Henry Morgan. The company on the mizzen deck huddled together as brothers, keen to hear the old salt's story.

Jack Bride, for that was the sailor's name, lifted his head back with glee at each murderous detail in his account of the war in the Spanish colonies. For that is how these pirates saw it, a war against the possessors of wealth. Whether they be Spanish, French, Dutch or even English, to these sea robbers it did not matter: if there was gain to be had, these villains were ready for the taking. And the marks of this war were in Jack Bride's eyes; cold, hard, as black as the pearl of San Luis.

He tossed his head back once again, his long grey beard glistening under the stars as he gave his account of the sacking of the town of Portobello; the looting of innocent homes, the rape of helpless mothers and the quartering of every man standing. These were the highlights of Jack Bride's war and his audience were spared nothing. They all listened in silence, not one man daring to take his leave until the murdering sea-dog had related every sickening detail.

But Toby was alone amongst these men, lost in his own thoughts. Could it be true that his father had been in Jamaica all this time? After all the years he had given to his search, the very reason he had come out to the colonies in the first place. The advertisement in the London broadsheet was a gift sent to him from God; *He that's a tradesman here in Mary-Land, lives as well as most common handicrafts do in London.*

Of course it was no coincidence that Toby had chosen the neighbouring colony to where his father had been posted. But surely this could not be the only reason for taking the long and hazardous journey: a voyage across the ocean to a land which promised little but hardship to search for a father who he had not seen or heard from since the age of ten? No, if he was honest, the decision to leave England was an escape from something far worse than an absent father. It was an escape from the memory of that fateful day when all that Toby ever loved had been taken from him. How could he continue living with the constant reminder of it all? He had to go, to begin a new life in a new land.

And what of his father? Would he care that his son was alive? Did the man have no curiosity about the fate of the family he had left behind? And what cause had he to desert them in the first place? Was allegiance to his King so important that it took precedence over the welfare of all those who loved him?

It had gone quiet on deck. Bride had finished his gruesome tale and his audience had now departed. Toby decided to take advantage of his disposition.

"The man Hopkins, you spoke of," he ventured.

"Aye?" Bride gave Toby a sideways glance.

"Can you say how old he was at the time?"

The man ran his fingers through a grey matted beard then pressed the flask to his lips. As he threw back his head the sharp point of an Adam's apple ran along the hamstrings of his weather-beaten neck. Bride let out a long deep belch.

"Bout the same as I," he said.

"Can you recall how tall?"

The old dog downed the last dreg and held out his empty flask. "My memory be as dry as my throat, boy."

Toby took his own flask from his pocket and poured Bride a shot.

"An officer in the militia, as I remember rightly," he said. "Stood a good hand taller than I."

This caught Toby's attention. An officer! "Was there any feature about him that was unusual?"

Again Bride held out his flask. Toby measured out half his ration.

"T'were on that fated ship, *The Trident*. T'was as if Neptune had a curse on us." The man stared out across the dark seas lost in his thoughts. After a minute Toby considered whether he should shake the old dog when he suddenly came back to life. "S'pose you be talking bout his ear then," he continued. "Like it be bitten off by a dog, ain't that so?"

Toby was speechless. He took a swallow from the flask and allowed the sweet syrup to seep through his veins. Intoxicated enough by what he had been told, he passed over the remainder of his ration to the pirate in the hope that it might extricate an answer to his final question.

"Can you tell me where I might find Mister Hopkins?"

Tucking the flask into his belt, the old sailor raised himself up and rested both hands on the hatch coving. There was the stench of death on his clothes.

"Your Mister *Hopskins* boarded with us at Port Royal." The pirate shook his head. "A fated trip, if ever there was."

"Fated? Why was that?"

"No sooner had we sailed out of Portobello an' were headed back for home, the bounty were gone. All our takings – gold, silver, stones, every man's share, gone an' vanished in the night."

"How did that happen?" Toby asked.

But Bride was gone. Toby watched him stagger towards the foredeck and steady himself against the gunwale. For several minutes the old salt stood there shaking his head as he stared into the black waters. Eventually, as if all energy had drained from him, the man dropped onto a stack of canvas stowed against the bulkhead. Those were the last words he heard from Jack Bride, for three days after they docked in Jamaica the man was murdered for little more than a shilling.

Toby rested back against the hatch and searched the bright stars above his head. Was his whole life destined to be taken up with rebuilding a string of shattered dreams? Each time he appeared to be on the right path, the ground would open up before him and swallow up all he had ever worked for. First there was the little house in Saint Mary; every frame crafted by himself – only to be swept away in the flood of seventy-three. Then there was the tobacco crop that had taken three seasons to mature – set alight and destroyed by that band of native savages. And now his beautiful brig, *The Chesapeake Venture*. Not only had Toby been forced to take her to Tortuga, he also had to watch her hull being ripped apart. And all for what? Just so those French butchers could mount twelve canons along her flanks and use his crew to assist them in their raids on the Spanish Main. And, after all they had gone through, the brigantine now lay resting in peace beneath the Bay of Maracaibo. If Toby hadn't been so easily impressed by the few words of an old hag with pretensions of witchery none of this would have happened.

With all the events over the past few weeks Toby had almost forgotten about that widow in Plymouth Colony. 'Take your quest to the English Isle in the Caribee Sea,' she had said. And like a lost lamb Toby followed her every word. No sooner was *The Chesapeake* seaworthy, he enlisted more hands and, against all advice, immediately set a course for Barbados. Would he have come all this way had he not been so taken with these words? Of course not. After all, he had given up all hope of finding his father years before. Piracy in this region is notorious, but did he take heed to the dangers? Not at all. And now, having lost so many of his crew, he would have to bear all responsibility.

A wisp of cloud, silvered by the moon, drifted past the bright star overhead.

'The English Isle in the Caribee Sea,' the widow had said.

Toby bolted upright from the hatch cover. He ignored the shot of pain along his right arm. Of course, the woman was referring to Jamaica, not Barbados! Strange words at the time, but now they make sense. Could it be, after all this time, after all these misfortunes, this may be a turning point in his life?

As Toby made his way back to his hammock, to the resting place where the dark veil of sleep waited to greet him, the thought of finally meeting his father filled his heart.

Chapter 3 – **The Colonel's Seat**

It had been four days since the raids on Maracaibo had ended and still the town of Port Royal had yet to hear the news. In the early hours of that Monday morning, about the time the Lady Charlotte caught first sight of the Island of Jamaica, the office of Fort Charles received the less welcome news that another high-ranking officer of the Jamaica militia had been murdered. It was reported that, at some time during the night, Colonel Thomas Wilcox-Brown had been stabbed to death by an intruder at his home in St. Jago. Sergeant Smithson and his assistant, Corporal Jones, were called in to investigate.

The journey from Port Royal to the old capital of Jamaica, St. Jago de la Vega, which some call Spanish Town, took a two mile ferry trip across the sheltered waters of Ripley Bay and another six mile trek inland. While Smithson could have hired a couple of mares when they disembarked at the dock, he was never that comfortable on horseback and chose to make the remainder of the journey on foot. After the first twenty minutes he regretted it. Not only did he have to contend with the oppressive humidity, but the track was festooned with all manner of obstacles: potholes, rocks, even fallen trees. It was one month since the hurricane and, apart from a couple of deadwood fires, little had been done to clear away the debris. Back in Port Royal everything was shipshape within two days. No matter what people said, thought Smithson, there was nothing appealing about living in the countryside. Nor could his assistant convince him. During the ferry trip Corporal Jones had been singing the praises of rural living – how good it would be to get away from the stifling streets of Port Royal, what a change it would be to breathe the country air again. The man was so jovial about the assignment you'd think they had boarded a vessel bound for the green fields of England – or, in *his* case, the grey-green valleys of Glamorganshire.

To Sergeant Smithson the countryside is somewhere where there is no town. At the next fire he stopped to rest his heavy frame against an uprooted palm tree. He took out his pipe and glanced at the road ahead.

"How much further by your reckoning, Jones?"

"Eh? What's that Sarge?" Corporal Jones was standing at the edge of the track, looking out across the valley.

Smithson shook the front of his sweat-soaked shirt in an attempt to circulate some cool air around his chest and wished they'd hired the horses. "How far away are we from St Jago, do you reckon, Jones?"

"Oh, I'd say we're almost half way there now, Sir."

Smithson sighed and set a tinder to his pipe. He wished he'd never agreed to take on this assignment (not that they had given him the choice). The investigation was becoming more of a mystery as time moved on and didn't seem to be heading for any kind of resolution.

Almost four years had gone by since the murders began and still there was nothing to show who the perpetrators were, or why such gruesome killings had taken place. And now the militia office was pushing Smithson to come up with some answers. Of course many officers stationed in Jamaica have met with an untimely fate over the years, but there had been none so cruel as the Cooper case back in seventy-one. That is, not until earlier this year when the whole business started up again.

Apart from the one they were about to see today, the most recent case happened back in July, just a few doors from the Governor's Mansion in Port Royal. Captain Rogers was in fact a retired officer.

The sergeant turned to his assistant. "Can you recall what day of the week it was that Rogers was killed?"

Corporal Jones sat down on a rock and opened his bag. He pulled out a bundle of papers and laid them in his lap.

"It's down here somewhere, Sarge." He flicked through the pages. "Ah, here it is. Seventeenth of July, that'll be . . . a Wednesday, Sir."

"So, no connection with the date. Nor the day of the week." Smithson scratched his side whiskers. "You got any reference in those scribblings as to when the gentleman retired from the militia?"

Jones flicked through the documents and pulled out a paper. "This is the one, I think." He ran his finger down the page and stopped at the last paragraph. "Ah yes, here we are. Captain Rogers only remained in service for three years after his commission. He retired in sixty-one and became a sugar merchant." The corporal looked up. "And a very prosperous business it seems, if you don't mind me saying, Sarge."

"Not a very happy ending though, eh, Jones?"

"I suppose not, Sir."

Rogers had been discovered in the attic of his fine house in Queen Street. In the same room was his valet, a Mr Jacobs, who had been stripped to the waist to endure a long and slow death at the mercy of a blade. The methods were almost identical to those suffered by Cooper and his wife four years earlier. The only difference was that Cooper had been finished off with a pistol shot to the head while Captain Rogers had ended his ordeal by having his throat severed. It was these events that concerned the Militia and Smithson was assigned to investigate the case.

The Sergeant tapped out the remains from his pipe against the tree and within seconds smoke started to billow from dry flaxen husks. He leapt up from his perch and cursed the God-forsaken countryside as he stamped out the flame. Giving Jones a cursory glance, he raised his eyes up to the heavens. "Come on Corporal, best we get going."

It was almost an hour later when, to Smithson's great relief, the rough track merged into a cobbled street at the southern edge of St. Jago de la Vega. The two investigators took a rest on a stone wall.

"So this is why they call it Spanish Town." Jones was looking up at the buildings in the street. "I suppose there must have been some Spanish settlers who came to live in this part of the island."

"Oh, so you haven't been briefed about this place?"

"Spanish Town?"

Smithson picked up a stick and began to poke the bowl of his pipe. "I was thinking of Jamaica. Someone should have told you a bit of history 'bout the island."

"I only arrived here November last year. I haven't been anywhere outside Port Royal."

The Sergeant tapped his pipe against the top of the wall. "Well, the English – and the Welsh, I should say, have only been in

Jamaica for the past twenty years. Before that it was occupied by the Spanish."

"This town?"

"The whole of Jamaica. This town was their capital."

Jones looked around at the buildings which seemed to show little sign of any damage. "Was there much resistance?"

"Hardly any from the Spaniards. Most ran off to Cuba like scared rats and left their servants and slaves behind to do the fighting. . . which, of course, they still do now."

"The Maroons?"

"Aye, and a thorn in the side they are too." Smithson tucked away his pipe and got up from the wall. "Come on Corporal, we've got work to do."

The two investigators set a brisk pace through the main Plaza and headed for the north side of the town.

They found Villa Paisaje at the far end of D'Oyley Street. The clerk who had been expecting them went to call the town constable as soon as they arrived. Having been woken and posted at the front of the house since the early hours of the morning, the man didn't look his best. As soon as he was gone Smithson stepped back to take another look at the impressive façade. Whilst a few of the original buildings in this part of St Jago had been destroyed during the English invasion, this was one fine example of the town's Spanish colonial past. The previous victim's home back in Queen Street may have been handsome but this one could only be described as grand: a pillared portico extending at least twenty feet to each side of the main entrance supported another balcony on the floor above. The walls of the villa were covered with white stucco plaster and the roof tiled with terracotta, probably imported from Portugal or Spain. Colonel Thomas Wilcox-Brown may have met with an untimely death but he certainly did well for himself while he was alive. A pity his residence had to be all the way out here.

The clerk returned, weary and bedraggled. Accompanying him was the town constable; the first man at the scene when the alarm was raised.

"Sergeant Smithson?" The constable looked from one to the other.

"That'll be me, Sir." Smithson turned to show the stripes on his sleeve.

"I understand you have been assigned to this case?"

"I have."

"Well, I suppose you'll want to take a look." The man was clearly reluctant at having to hand the investigation over to the militia.

"Before we do that, if you don't mind. Sir," Smithson said. "Can you tell me in your own words what happened here?"

"Colonel Brown has been murdered."

"Yes, I understand that. But can you tell me who raised the alarm?"

"Mathilde, er, she's the Colonel's parlour-maid."

"I see. And what time would that be, Sir?"

"A little after four this morning."

"Was she the one who found the body?"

"I believe so, Sergeant."

Smithson turned to his assistant. "Do you have that, Jones?"

"Aye, Sarge."

Smithson waited for Corporal Jones to make a note with his new graphite stick. He looked up at the man at the door. "Is there anything else you think we should know, Sir?"

"Well Sergeant. . . " The Constable puffed up his chest. "It is my belief that the perpetrator entered the property through a window in the pantry. Apart from that, you should be warned that the scene is not a pleasant sight." It was clear the Constable was pleased with himself.

"One more thing. How many others are present here, other than yourself and your clerk of course?"

"Just the maid and the houseboy."

"Where are they now?"

"I've asked them to wait in the parlour. They've been there for nearly four hours now, Sergeant. Matilde is very disturbed by the whole thing."

"Yes, I'm sure." Smithson frowned at the stick scratching its way across the paper beside him.

Jones always insisted on bringing these items along whenever they were sent out on an investigation and the sergeant was convinced it was only to make a good impression. He turned back to the constable. "Apart from yourself and the servants, has anyone else entered the room where the crime was committed?"

"No, Sergeant. Not as far as I am aware."

"Fine, thank you, Sir." Smithson looked toward the clerk who had resumed his position on the bench at the end of the portico. The man could hardly keep his eyes open and his head was continually dropping to his chest. "Would it be possible to relieve your clerk and have someone posted here for today?"

"I'm sure that's possible. I'll arrange it now, Sergeant."

Smithson waited until the constable was out of earshot.

"Now Jones, I want you to go gentle with the girl. See if you can find out if the master of the house had any unusual callers lately. We don't know what we'll find in here, but I suspect there'll be much out of place. Ask them both if anything has been touched or removed." He ran his hand through his whiskers. "They've been waiting a long time in there. It would be an idea if you went around the house with them room by room, but be sure they don't touch anything, is that clear?"

"Aye, Sarge."

The constable returned. "I've sent him home, Sergeant. Someone will be here in about half an hour to replace him."

"Well, Constable, I think we should go in and take a look."

As soon as they entered the house the steady click from a grand timepiece which stood proud at the end of the hall caught their attention. Jones was particularly taken with the workings of the mechanism. Smithson made a note of the time.

The Constable led the way to the cellar, where the lamp exposed damp blackened walls pinned with dark beams dressed with abandoned spider webs. As they ventured further into the room the light scattered a pack of marauding cockroaches across the earth and stone floor. The coolness, in comparison to the humidity outside, was a welcome change. However, the dampness clung to the skin and, even if unaware of recent events, bestowed a foreboding air in which one could sense the taint of death.

A chair had been placed at the centre of the room and under the flickering flame of the oil-lamp, the body seated in it wouldn't necessarily arouse suspicion. Dressed in his undershirt and pantaloons, one might assume the Colonel to be sleeping off a heavy bout of drinking. The presence of two empty wine bottles discarded at the man's feet and the stains on his clothing would further suggest this. It is only on closer inspection that one could see something was not right. The man's arms had been forced into an unnatural position behind the back of the chair. His face, pale and drained, drooped forward with his chin resting on his chest.

It was the manner in which the Colonel had been secured to the chair which first caught Smithson's attention; a heap of knots obviously tied by someone who had not the first idea of what they were doing. And that was not the only difference. Both the previous victims had concluded their ordeal with a quick and efficient end; Cooper with a pistol shot to the head and Rogers with a clean cut across the throat. Here, in the quiet seclusion of Colonel Brown's cellar, the poor man had been stabbed to death by a maniac. So many times had the weapon entered the victim's body, and in such a clumsy manner, that the perpetrator must have had little confidence in his abilities as a murderer, or else he must have been in a rage.

For about three to four feet around the chair, the floor was awash with blood. Much of which had now soaked into the clay leaving an array of boot impressions. The sergeant placed his own shoe alongside a particularly clear imprint. Smithson took an extraordinarily large boot size for himself (a matter which always presented him with difficulties when looking for suitable footwear) but this particular print was several sizes smaller and suggested that the villain would be slight in stature, or at least reasonably slim.

Smithson turned to the constable who was standing some way back from the scene. "Would you be so good and give some light on the poor gentleman please?"

Averting his eyes from the figure, the constable took a pace closer and held up the lamp.

"This won't take long, Sir," said Smithson.

The chair had been placed at the centre of the room and under the flickering flame of the oil-lamp, the body seated in it made a chilling sight. Dressed in his undershirt and pantaloons, one could assume the Colonel to be sleeping off a heavy bout of drinking. The presence of two empty wine bottles discarded at the man's feet and the stains on his clothing would further suggest this. It was on closer inspection that one could see something was not right. The man's arms had been forced into an unnatural position behind the back of the chair. His face, pale and drained, drooped forward with his chin resting on his chest.

Sergeant Smithson took a step forward. He attempted to pull the man's head back but it was impossible to move it. He squatted down and searched within the folds of flesh under the Colonel's chin but there was no sign of any cuts. The victim's eyes which had now taken on the colour of watered milk, stared unseeing into his own. Smithson straightened up. He next took the tail of the Colonel's undershirt. The cotton material, caked in congealed blood, pulled at the man's flesh as he lifted it away. The incisions were made by a wide blade, possibly the kind used for kitchen work. But what was more revealing, and particularly relevant to this case, was the absence of any marks which would have indicated that the man had been tortured during his ordeal.

A shadow was cast over the corpse.

The constable, who had been holding the lamp for the past few minutes, had now let it drop to his side. Face pale and eyes wide in horror he was staring at the man in the chair.

Smithson let the shirt fall back to cover the victim's body. "Well, that'll do for now, Constable. We've finished down here."

Corporal Jones was sitting at the oak table in the kitchen. Across from him was Matilde, a girl of eighteen and the boy, Jack, who had recently turned ten. The girl seemed nervous when Smithson and the constable entered the room; her eyes rimmed red as if she had been crying. The sergeant decided to let her be for the moment and headed for the door of the pantry. As soon as he rounded the table he was greeted with a threatening growl. A large dog appeared from the far side of the room. Smithson slipped into the pantry and just managed to close the door in time. He breathed in the aroma of fruits and salted meats which had also attracted several flies which were buzzing around the shelves. The space was quite narrow but by squeezing his way along he reached a small window which opened out onto the garden at the rear of the house. The frame, along with its insect netting, had been removed from the outer housing. However, nothing was certain in Smithson's mind until it was proven. He called for his assistant to remove the dog and bring the parlour-maid.

"Now Matilde, can you say how long this window has been like this?"

The girl seemed genuinely surprised to see the damage and confirmed that it was not in that condition the day before. She also expressed her concern that the food was exposed to pests.

Smithson assured her that he and Corporal Jones would replace the netting before they depart.

He then asked Jones to accompany him to the garden and on their way out asked the girl to lock the door behind them. The window frame had been placed against the wall of the house a few feet away from the point of entry and a wooden crate positioned on the ground immediately below the opening. Jones picked up the frame and was about to return it to its rightful place when the sergeant held up his hand.

"Before you do that, Jones, I want you to climb through there and make your way to the kitchen."

"Through there Sarge? Why don't I go back through the door, Sir?"

"Just bear with me, son."

Smithson stood back and watched the slim figure of his assistant squeeze through the tiny opening. It was with some difficulty that he eventually disappeared into the pantry. Moments later the door lock turned and Jones appeared with a perplexed expression.

"Why did you want me to do that, Sarge?" Jones pointed to the opening in the wall. "We both know the villain got into the house through there."

"Yes Jones, I'm sure you're right. But is everyone as slim as you?"

"No, Sir."

"And was it not an arduous task to get through that tiny opening?"

"T'was that. Yes."

"In that case, would you not say that the person who entered this property could not be any larger than yourself?"

Jones nodded in agreement and they both set to the task of replacing the frame in its position. Before returning to the house the Sergeant took his assistant aside. "How are you getting along with those two in there?"

"The girl is hiding something, I'm sure."

"What makes you say that?"

"Whenever I ask if she heard or seen anything during the night she breaks down and weeps."

"Well, keep trying. There may be something." Smithson ran his fingers through his beard. "Where did that hound come from?"

"Upstairs in the Colonel's bed chamber. When the girl opened the door the dog ran out straight down the stairs to the kitchen."

The sergeant frowned. "Surely someone would have heard a dog barking in the middle of the night."

"I'll look into it, Sir."

"Did you see anything unusual in the Colonel's room?"

"The bed cover was pulled onto the floor, as if he had been disturbed from his sleep."

"Anything missing?"

"The girl had a good look around. Nothing had gone, but she said his desk was untidy."

"Have you looked in any of the other rooms?"

"Not yet, Sarge. They wanted to come down to feed the dog."

"That's fine. I'm going to inspect that outbuilding over there. See if you can find out what it is that's worrying the girl. I'll take a look around the house when I've finished."

The outbuilding had nothing to offer in the way of clues and Sergeant Smithson returned to find the kitchen empty. He inspected the rooms along the passage which led from there. The first had a small bed, two dresses hanging from a peg and a few female items hidden away in a box in the corner. This was obviously the girl's room. Considering the events which had taken place during the night, Smithson thought it strange that the bed was made and the place was very tidy. He moved further down the corridor.

At first sight, the next room appeared to be a laundry cupboard. Most of the floor-space was taken by a large basket filled with various items of clothing apparel. There was little else of note apart from a boy's jerkin which had been discarded in the corner. The Sergeant stood in the doorway and sniffed the air. He closed his eyes and took in the fresh aroma of newly washed linen. He was about to leave when he noticed a bed-board onto which a linen sheet had been thrown.

Back along the corridor he had another look in the girl's room. Strange the the maid had chosen to make up her bed that morning. He made a note to ask the girl.

He found the others sitting quietly in the parlour, the room at the front of the house where the two servants had been waiting when they first arrived. The town constable was filling out his report at the table and Jones was with the two servants making notes. Smithson asked the girl to show him around the upper floor of the house.

The Colonel's bed chamber was positioned directly above the girl's room; another fact which further puzzled Smithson. However, everything here was as Jones had described it: bed stripped of its covers and desk in disarray. Resting on the ledge above the fireplace stood a gold chalice; the same as seen in the churches of Spanish Catholics. Smithson turned to the girl.

"Has this been placed here this morning?"

"No, Sir. It were always there, Sir." Her reply was accompanied with a respectful curtsy.

"And the dog, where does it sleep at night?"

"She sleeps on the master's bed, Sir."

"Now, Matilde, look around carefully. Do you notice anything missing from this room, apart from items from the desk, that is?" He watched the girl closely as she pursued every corner of the room.

"No, Sir. Everything is as it should be, Sir." She followed her statement with another curtsy.

Along the corridor there was another door which was locked.

"Where is the key for this room, Matilde?"

The girl looked down to the floor. "The master wishes nobody to go in there, Sir."

"That's all right, Matilde," Smithson assured her. "I'm sure he would have wanted us to look into this as closely as possible."

The maid thought about this for a moment, then walked over to the far end of the hall where a vase stood alone on a small table. She reached her hand inside and brought out a small iron key which turned smoothly in the lock. The girl was about to reach for the handle when Smithson stopped her.

"Have you noticed this before?" The sergeant pointed to a splintered section of the door frame close to the lock.

"No, I haven't, Sir."

Smithson stroked his chin thoughtfully. "There is one thing which I am puzzled about, Matilde." He looked hard at the girl. "Your sleeping quarters, I note, are directly below these rooms, are they not?"

The girl looked down at her feet and nodded.

"What puzzles me," Smithson continued. "With all this commotion, such as the dog barking and doors and windows being forced, how come you did not hear any of it?"

Smithson noticed the colour rise to the girl's cheeks.

"I dunno, Sir," she mumbled, putting up her hands to cover her face.

"Now, come, come, my girl." The sergeant placed his arm across her shoulder. "There's no call to go upsetting yourself. I'll tell you what we'll do. Let's go and sit in the kitchen and talk over a nice mug of ale, yes?"

The maid nodded and the sergeant led the way back to the kitchen. Once they were settled at the table, Smithson took out his pipe and filled it from a leather pouch. He glanced up at the girl. "Where was young Jack when you got back this morning?"

Matilde sat quietly fiddling with her hands in her lap.

"There's no need to worry yourself now. You're not going to be in any trouble for taking an evening off from your duties once in a while."

The girl hesitated but still offered no reply.

"And your master is in no position to punish you for that now, is he?"

"He were hidin' in the laundry box." Her words, almost a whisper.

"Jack?"

She nodded.

"Ah, I see. He must have been very frightened then."

"He were shaking all over when I find him." The maid looked up as the sergeant set a flame to his pipe. Her eyes followed the billowing clouds of smoke rising to the ceiling.

"Did he tell you what happened?" Smithson asked.

"He said he went to get a piece of bread from the kitchen and that's when he heard a load of noise comin' from the cupboard 'ere." She nodded towards the pantry. "He were so frightened that he just sneaked off back to his room, an that's when he hears voices –"

"What voices?" The sergeant looked across at the girl.

"I dunno, just said there was voices, talkin' quiet like in the passage. That's when he buried his-self in the washing basket."

"Did he say they were men's voices?"

"Nah, I don't think he did. Shall I ask him?"

"No, that's no matter, Matilde. I'll ask him later." Smithson took a few sucks on his pipe, went over to the stove and set another light to it.

"Did Jack stay in the wash basket until you got back?"

"Yes, Sir."

"What time would that be?" Smithson looked hard at the girl. "Now think about this carefully, Matilde. Can you remember?"

There was a long pause while the girl stared at her cup on the table.

"I think it were about four, Sir."

"Are you sure about that?"

"Yes, Sir. It must have been 'cos I looks at the clock in the hall before I goes to fetch Mister Taylor and it say it was ten past the hour by then."

"Was that after you found the Colonel?"

"Yes, Sir."

"How did you find him?"

"Jack told me."

"So when did Jack discover the body?"

Matilde frowned. "Oh, I dunno. He didn't tell me that."

"No?" Smithson watched the girl's puzzled expression.

"Strange that he never told me," she added.

"Well, that's fine." Smithson placed his pipe on the table and ran his hand across his face. "A couple more questions, Matilde. Can you tell me where you were last night?"

The girl looked down at her cup and shuffled her feet.

"This is very important." The Sergeant prompted.

"I was at my Charlie's house."

"Charlie?"

"He's my fiancé, we're due to be wed next month."

"I see. And what time did you leave here to visit him?"

"Just after eleven, after Master Brown retired for the night."

"How often do you have a night away from the house?"

"Never, Sir. Well, not official like."

"And unofficial?"

"Just once a week… to see my Charlie."

"Every Monday?"

"Yes, Sir."

"One more thing. Could you look around here and tell me if you notice anything missing?"

The sergeant re-lit his pipe while the maid inspected the contents of cupboards and drawers in the kitchen.

"Nothing missing, Sir." She glanced along the worktop. "Oh now, wait one minute. There's a knife gone from the rack 'ere."

Smithson blew a stream of smoke in the air. "Can you describe it for me?"

"Well, it's the big one I use for cutting the meat, 'bout this long." The maid held her hands apart.

"And the blade. How wide would that be?"

"Oh, wide enough. Like so." The space between the girl's fingers was at least three inches.

"Thank you, Matilde. You may go back and join the others in the parlour now."

Sergeant Smithson waited until the girl had gone then headed for the stairs.

The locked room on the landing turned out to be a study; much smaller than he expected, with a little window overlooking the front of the house and a view of the town. The room was furnished with a writing desk and high back wooden chair. It was ten minutes past eleven when Smithson sat at the desk. He meticulously went through the documents filed in each drawer of the desk. Amongst the papers were a number of embarkation lists which related to the privateering raids on Portobello led by Lieutenant Governor Henry Morgan in sixty-eight. One such list, referring to the company mustered on *The Trident*, included the names of the murder victims Cooper and Rogers. The sergeant took a quill and paper from the desk and copied down all the names from this list. When he had finished, he checked that everything was as he found it, locked the door and returned downstairs.

While the search may have been enlightening, the knowledge he had gained by making these discoveries placed him in a rather uncomfortable position. Many of the documents indicated that

Colonel Thomas Wilcox-Brown had been the most senior link between the Governor of Jamaica and all privateering activities in the Western Caribbean. He had been the man responsible for issuing "Letters of Marque" to any pirate operations which the English government thought worthy of association. He was also responsible for the collection of duties and taxes on all bounty taken during these operations and had the authority to issue fines and punishments to those who did not comply. The papers also included Henry Morgan who had only this past year been appointed Lieutenant Governor of Jamaica. While much of this information was relevant to the case, nearly all of it was classified as confidential. Should he use what he had learnt today as evidence in solving these murders, or should he keep it to himself? That was his dilemma.

Corporal Jones was waiting on the front porch when the sergeant came down. In the course of his interview with the houseboy he discovered that Jack had crept out of his hiding place at some time during the early hours, but as soon as he saw the Colonel down in the cellar he immediately returned to the wash basket. The poor boy must have been terrified, for it was at least another hour before Matilde returned to the house and found him.

It was now a quarter before noon. Their task at Villa Paisaje was finished. As the sergeant and his assistant stepped down from the porch, a distant canon fire resounded across Ripley Bay to welcome the return of yet another group of marauders. The restrictions on privateering over the past few years seemed to have little effect: this was the third fleet to sail into the harbour in the last month. The two men looked at each other knowing that their return to Port Royal would now be hampered by the crowds amassed at the quayside.

Chapter 4 – The Merchant's Inn

The smoke on the horizon could be seen long before the town came into view. Attracted by the distant sound of canon fire, Toby had been standing at the starboard rail of the forecastle since first light. There were two vessels ahead of the Lady Charlotte. As the second rounded the point of the harbour, another sharp crack resounded across the bay. Seconds later a cloud of white smoke drifted over the rooftops of the town. This was Toby's first view of Jamaica, and the town of Port Royal was indeed a strange sight to behold.

Set against a backdrop of blue-hazed mountains, the seeds of the town had been planted on the tip of a peninsula which projected like a crooked finger from the eastern end of the Bay of St Andrews. The town, crammed atop an outcrop of coral and sand, was parted from the mainland by means of a narrow spit colonised by mangroves. Two churches were visible on the seaward approach, each jostled for some peace and solitude from the houses and streets which spilled out to the water's edge. Three forts dominated the southern approach; a defence to remind all visitors that this town was the most formidable port in the Caribbean Sea.

The first to greet the Lady Charlotte as she approached to port was a gang of seabirds intent of scrounging whatever came in sight of their bright orange eyes and whatever could be carried of in their sharp yellow beaks. The birds, disappointed by their unsuccessful venture, took vengeance on two of the crew stationed at the topgallant spar. The conflict became so intense that the cook took it in mind to race down to the galley and return with a bucket topped up with what remained of the ships sea biscuits. He tossed the whole lot over the side and called up to the offending birds, "Get that down yer gizzards if ye can and I hope it chokes you!" This did the job as the flock detached themselves from the two men aloft and dived onto the offering in one giant splash twenty feet off the stern.

The wind dropped to a light air as the vessel rounded the point at Fort Charles. Another shot was fired from the west wall of the fort to welcome the Lady Charlotte into the harbour. In all the ports he had traded, never had Toby seen one so busy as this one. Vessels of every design were moored out into the bay and many more were docked right up to the quayside. So numerous were they that it would have been impossible to count them in one sitting.

The Lady Charlotte was the third vessel of their fleet to arrive at the port and news of their successful mission had preceded them. A huge crowd had gathered on the quayside; rogues dressed in rags stood alongside gentlemen suited in finery, whores with little but the most meagre of apparel pressed against society ladies attired in the latest fashions. There was a great deal of pushing and shoving and it seemed the whole town had come out to wave and cheer the vessel as she drew up alongside.

With arms folded, Toby leant against the gunwale of the main deck and studied the gathering ashore. Less concerned was he for recognition of any heroic deed, he declined to return their greetings even with the slightest wave, nor did he raise his hand in acknowledgement of their applause. Instead, Toby searched the face of every man in the crowd. Should any head be taller than the rest, or should a flash of red tunic catch his attention, Toby would fix his eye on that figure like a hawk.

"What's the plan, Captain?" The Mate of the fateful *Chesapeake*, in cheerful spirit, was standing beside him.

"What? Ah yes, Mister Fowler, you're quite right, we ought have an appointment in mind." Toby turned back to face the crowd.

"Some welcome, eh Sir?"

The captain didn't reply. John tried to engage his attention. "Would it be best we meet at that alehouse over there, Captain?"

Toby gave a cursory glance toward a tavern dwarfed between two capacious warehouses. "Yes, that's fine."

The crew were now beginning to disembark and John was eager to join them. "With respect, Captain, you didn't say a time."

Toby sighed. He tried to estimate how long he would need to procure a new vessel. "Shall we say in four days? Oh, I don't know… midday?"

"Aye Captain, noon on Friday then."

John Fowler headed off to join his shipmates who were now calling from the dock. At the head of the gangplank, he turned back to his captain. "You not going ashore, Sir?"

"What? Oh yes, in a while."

Toby watched the Mate, a man he had known for more than five years, push his way through the crowd to join his comrades. From the first day he took him on, John Fowler had always been popular amongst the crew. Yet, considering his rank, this familiarity never seemed to bear any consequence. It often occurred to Toby that he should warn him to take a more distant stance from the other hands, but somehow he was always inclined to drop the idea.

It was just after midday when the last of the crew had gone ashore. The sun was directly overhead when Toby crossed the gangplank. The gold chalice and silver plates gave an audible clunk as he slung his kit bag over his shoulder and headed for the town. The tavern they had observed from the vessel was called *The Spar and Halyard* and, judging from the raucous noise from inside, this was where most of the crew had now stationed themselves. Toby quickened his pace as he passed by the windows of the inn.

Following the path of the crowd from the jetty, he took the next turning south; a rather dismal alley which led to a promising thoroughfare at the far end. Before venturing down this side street Toby dropped the bag from his shoulder, took off his hat and wiped the sweat from his brow. Not wishing to provoke unwanted attention he tucked the pistol into the front of his belt and fastened his tunic over the butt.

Most of the buildings along the passage were modest timber-framed domestic structures, many with their shutters open to allow the putrid air of the alley to circulate within. Some of the women of these meagre dwellings were fanning themselves at their windows, others stood in doorways conversing with neighbours. Most eyed Toby with some curiosity as he made his way along the passage, some even making comment as he passed them by. Halfway along the alley an old hag, dressed in a thin linen petticoat, was resting her fleshy arms at her window. Toby stopped as she greeted him.

"Good day to you, Madam. Would you be so kind as to direct me to an inn?"

The woman looked over to her neighbour across the way. "An *in*, did he say?" she laughed. "Never heard it called that before."

Turning back to Toby, the hag gave him a toothless smile and nodded toward the front of his tunic. "But I can see you're pleased to see me, my lovely."

Toby quickly adjusted the position of the pistol butt under his tunic.

"Never mind her." The neighbour stepped down from her doorway. "Try the Merchant's in York Street." She pointed towards the end of the passageway. "Right into Queens, take a left when you get to Lime. York Street is right down past the fish market, on the left."

The old woman at the window started up again. "An' if you get lost, you be welcome to come *in* here any time, my sugar," her words echoing through the narrow alley as Toby hurried from the scene.

The road at the end of the alley, which her friend called *Queens*, was deserted; not a soul to be seen, a wide thoroughfare flanked by houses above a carpet of dry white dust. Toby screwed his eyes and waited until he could take in the buildings which framed the shimmering road. Wooden dwellings that were little more than shacks and shops with windows barred with iron huddled close to solid brick-built buildings in an effort to seek shade from the baking sun. Some of the more substantial houses were at least three floors high. It was as if the heart of an English town had been taken from its moorings and shipped to a tropical wasteland.

There was not a soul in sight and no sign of any place to stay, any building that looked remotely like a lodging house had its shutters firmly closed. If there had not been a gathering to welcome the Lady Charlotte when she docked, one would believe the town to be abandoned.

With the bag weighing heavily on his shoulder, the soles of his feet burning in the sand and the humidity soaking his shirt, Toby trudged his way westward leaving a cloud of dust to settle onto the road behind him. The air was oppressive, tainted with the odour of human waste, at times so strong that Toby had to hold the sleeve of his shirt against his face.

After a few paces he reached a shop which advertised salted beef and various pickled meats. Exhausted, he dropped the bag to the ground and took a rest. It was here he met the only other traveller along this lonely highway; a solitary cockroach the size of a snuffbox. Toby raised his hat and bid the little creature 'Good day'. However, taking objection to the obstacles in its path, the insect had already set off on a new course, its spindle legs rippling through the soft sand until it negotiated a way around the kitbag and disappeared into a crack along the shop wall.

A movement in the doorway caught Toby's eye; a tarnished silver buckle glinting in the sunlight. The buckle was attached to a gentleman's shoe, heeled in the finest hardwood, which projected out from the shop entrance. Toby gave the shoe a nudge with his toe. It retracted into the shadows. He moved closer to investigate. The body of a man, his face obscured under a large felt tricorn hat and a mass of dark ringlets, lay huddled in the corner. He nudged the foot again: this time the figure retreated. Both hat and periwig slipped to the floor during the scuffle and revealed an emaciated face of the palest complexion with red-rimmed eyes sunken deep into the skull.

"Please don't harm me. I have nothing to my name," the man croaked, white spittle clinging to the corners of his mouth.

"I mean you no harm, Sir," assured Toby. "I merely enquire if you know of a hostel that can accommodate me in this town?"

"I promise you, I am a poor man, fallen on hard times. If I had a penny I would give it to you. Please leave me in peace, I beg you."

While the man could speak perfect English, a slight accent coloured his phrases. It bothered Toby that he failed to identify it. "Can you tell me where there is an inn?" he repeated.

The man took up the wig and the hat, replaced them in the approximate region of his head and scrambled to his feet. He swayed a little, then, very slowly, slipped down to his knees. At the second attempt, and with the aid of the wall to support him, the man eventually stood up. However, in his enthusiasm he forgot to retain his hold and toppled forward against Toby's chest.

"An inn, you say?" The man's breath reeked of spirits.

Keeping him at arms length, Toby tried to steady him. "Yes, somewhere to stay."

"I know a good place where we can stay, and not far from here, friend. They serve a fine drop of brandy there too." Placing both hands to his forehead, the man drew back the curtain of curls and ringlets from his eyes. "Come with me, I'll show you."

Without waiting for a reply, Toby's new companion toppled forward and allowed the momentum of his body to project him up the street. Toby followed at a short distance, should the man again lose his balance. Somewhat confused with his bearings the drunkard meandered up and down the road for a good few minutes until, eventually, out of breath, he came to rest against the door of a house less than two buildings away from the shop where they started.

Before he could be stopped, the man began hammering incessantly at the door calling out for the owner to open up.

Toby started to walk away.

"What do you want?" An angry face shouted from the window above.

Toby's companion took two paces back from the door, looked up to the window, and promptly fell arse-first into the road.

"Oh, it's you!" the man at the window growled. "Heave off, before I come down there and cut your tongue out!" The shutters closed with a violent crash sending a scattering of dust over the two men in the street below.

Undeterred, the drunkard was back on his feet. He turned to Toby and promised he'd kick the door down to get them in. It took more than a little determination to persuade him to return to his original resting place. The whole arduous journey was repeated, this time complemented with warnings never to trust the word of a Dutchman. At last the man sank back into the entrance of the shop which sold pickled meats.

"You have a good heart, friend." He reached up to shake Toby's hand. "Angelo Guido, a pleasure to be at your service. And please, always remember to take heed of my advice."

So, the man is Italian, thought Toby. He thanked him for his good intentions, tipped his hat and continued his search. When he reached the end of the road he turned left. After passing the closed gates of the fish market, he took the second turning left into York Street. And there it was: The Merchant's Inn.

A hubbub of voices could be heard beyond the door as Toby approached, but as soon as he entered all went silent. Positioned in the centre of the dark hall was a rough looking group seated around a large oak table piled high with various vestments and apparel. At the head of the table stood a swarthy man who was holding up a gentleman's blue velvet jerkin.

"How can I help thee?" said the man, immediately allowing the item to drop to the pile.

All turned to fix their eyes on the stranger in their presence.

"Do you have a room that can accommodate me for the night?"

The request was repeated in whispers amongst the group.

The man, who had taken on the role of proprietor, looked Toby up and down. He then beckoned him over to the corner of the room where a large barrel leaked its contents onto the stone floor. He leaned over the barrel and took down an iron key from a hook on the wall. Before handing it over he made it clear that the rent was to be paid in advance. The supply of a wash basin and soap was added to the bill (a fare that would match any of the best lodging houses in London), and an excessive charge was made for a jug of brackish water. The day being far too hot to haul a heavy kitbag around town, Toby paid the fee.

All eyes watched the new guest in silence as he slipped the key and bar of soap into the pocket of his coat. But when he shifted his kit bag further onto his shoulder it made a clunk; a sound which drew more than a little interest from the group seated at the table. With the jug in his hand and basin tucked under his arm, Toby headed up the stairs. It was only when he turned the corner and was out of sight that the voices at the table resumed their babble.

For two flights up the narrow passage, he dragged these victuals, only to discover he had been assigned to a room in the attic. It was obvious that the key he had been given would never pass through the slot carved into the wood. However, as soon as he stepped forward, the door swung open and presented him with a space little more than the size of a cupboard.

The room was sparsely furnished. A bed of hard wooden boards took up most of the floor space and a shelf, crudely nailed to the wall, led to the room's most redeeming feature: a tiny window, positioned so high up, it could only offer a view of the sky above. At the best of times there was never enough air ashore and this attic offered no exception. The tropical sun bore down so fiercely onto the roof tiles the tiny room reminded Toby of those meat ovens he had left behind in Tortuga.

Toby placed the wash-basin, soap and water jug on the shelf, dropped his bag onto the narrow floor-space and went over to the window. In the vain hope that a southerly breeze from the coast might find its way to this part of town, he tried to open it. Only at the third attempt did the shutter give way, almost loosening its mooring and dropping to the street below. Toby peeled off his saturated clothes and washed himself. Standing naked in the centre of the floor, his body dripping with sweat, he squeezed as much of his apparel as could fit into the washbasin to soak. Exhausted after his efforts, he lay down onto the boards and closed his eyes. His first day ashore and he'd already had enough: he yearned to be back at sea again. Within minutes he was asleep.

The little girl skips through the fresh green grass – her face alive with excitement. Lily-pads, new and small, line the water's edge. The gentle surface of the river broken into a thousand sparkling jewels reflected in the morning sun. Rowers in skips glide through the silk water. Cheeks, alabaster smooth, eyes as bright as diamonds, the girl squeals with delight as she runs from her hiding place behind the elder-bush. She ducks beneath the curtain of a weeping willow tree, its silver green fronds brush through the grass about her feet. From a window in the branches above, her mother calls – her words silenced by the stillness of the day. A splash of oar on the river – a uniformed man puts his back into the pull as his skiff cuts through the water like a knife.

The mother at the window looks down in horror. Branches alight – a lick of flame rushes to the crest of the tree. The girl begins to cry. The skiff slides through the silver grey mist. A canon from the bank welcomes the rower. Flames like the tongues of dragons devour the boards of a timber bulkhead. A silver chalice, clean and bright, twists and folds into submission. Distant screams from the mother as tears channel through blackened cheeks of the girl. The officer salutes as he passes the gathering on the dock – smoke obscures the crowd in their frenzied rush. Lighted branches fall about the girl – her mother runs through the scorched grass – the girl is still – alabaster cheeks blister, eyes blacken – her mother screams, and screams, and screams.

Toby shot up from the boards, his skin tight with the horror of it all, the screams continuing to ring inside his head. He rubbed his face hard to bring himself awake and tried to make sense of the sounds invading his little attic room: a disturbance in the street below. He moved quickly to the window, squeezed his head through the tiny gap. For more than a minute he stood there listening to the desperate cries and abusive threats from the street. Then, for no apparent reason, they stopped. A scurry of steps ran along the alley adjacent to the lodging house. Toby returned to perch on the end of his bed-board.

The room was a little cooler than before; the sun now low in the sky. A few hours must have passed. How could he have wasted so much of the day! There was much to do. First he needed to find somewhere safe to deposit his booty. From all he had heard, Port Royal was not the place to carry a bag laden with valuables around at night.

He made haste to get dressed, then cursed – his clothes were still soaking in the basin. Now he would need to wring them out and waste another hour waiting for them to dry. He searched his bag and, as luck would have it, he found a clean pair of breeches and a thin cotton shirt stuffed down the side. Moments later Toby lifted the kitbag to his shoulder, took a glance at the various items of his apparel arranged around the room, pulled the door and headed down the stairs.

Chapter 5 – A Strange Society

It so happened that Port Royal supported as many financial houses as it did taverns and whore houses: each establishment offering a temporary service for a substantial fee. While Toby was relieved to leave the bulk of his valuables at a depository, he had a mission to accomplish and had no intention to visit any tavern or whore house. Based on the information given to him by the pirate, Jack Bride, he felt the need to follow up his story with an official enquiry at the Militia.

Fort Charles was situated on a promontory at the south-west corner of town; the military office standing within the austere walls of the fort. On hearing his request, the desk sergeant eyed Toby with suspicion. He offered very little information other than to confirm that a Capt. Edward James Hopkins was commissioned from Virginia between the years of 1662 and 1667. He could not, or rather would not, say what happened to him over the past eight years. In his view, all military personnel holding a rank higher than Sergeant were incompetent and therefore superfluous to the defence of the town. He also held the view that all civilians, merchants and sailors who visit Port Royal carry the same flag as the pirates and buccaneers who infest the streets of the town. A merchant seaman inquiring of the whereabouts of a military officer would surely be up to no good.

"Let me tell you something, lad." The sergeant leaned across his desk and lowered his voice. "All the officers here are buffoons. Rather than acquaint themselves with affairs of this garrison, most bide their time at the house of Madam Leticia. And thank God for that, I say!"

Taking heed of this advice, Toby headed back in search of the house of Madam Leticia.

Now that the intense heat of the day had elapsed, there was much activity in the town. People of every status jostled together in the street: it was as if all had come out of hiding. As Toby mingled among these people he could hear many languages; the most common being English, but French, Flemish and even Spanish were spoken freely.

To avoid the crowds, Toby took a turning off Lime Street which led to a sheltered bay where many small fishing craft were moored. The tranquil place with the sun setting over the distant hills was a welcome haven compared to the busy streets he had left behind. The track led him along the shoreline to a market place which traded, among other things, the sale of turtle meat. It was outside here that Toby came across what appeared to be a bear cage; a structure of about three by three cubits square with an entry door and walls of stout wooden poles. Nailed to the roof of the cage was a curious sign engraved with the words *'Lazie Strumpet'*.

"Good day, Sir." A bearded youth dressed in a ragged singlet and a pair of torn breeches had appeared alongside as if from nowhere. "You here for the sentencing?"

Toby was considering what this could mean when the young man continued.

"I could get you some ripe tomatoes at a good price, if you wish."

As this enlisted no response, the man tried another tack. "How about a slave to save you from the arduous tasks of the day? I can sell you a trusty man just arrived from Barbados." The youth cocked his head to one side in the hope that this would inspire a response.

Toby was reminded of the story of rebellious negroes escaping from that same island. "Forgive me, but I have little need for a servant. Thank you." With this he got no reply and when he turned to look at the man, he was gone. Peace at last.

However, it was not long before the tranquillity of the place was broken. A crowd had emerged from the streets of the town and was headed down an alley in Toby's direction. Leading the gathering were two burly gentlemen striding each side of a bare-footed female dressed in nothing but a linen petticoat. The woman, who had taken objection to being dragged along the street, was shouting abuse at her escorts and demanded to be released. When they reached the end of the lane a military man stepped out from the crowd and opened the door of the cage. He stood aside while the female was thrown into the structure then secured the door with a lock and chain. As soon as she picked herself up from the floor the woman pushed herself up to the bars and spat at the jeering crowd. One of her escorts held up a paper.

"Herewith at the hour of two in the morning of this day the twenty-ninth of September you, Jenny Comfort, didst at the Cheapside Tavern in Wherry Lane take a bottle and threaten a Mister Thomas Francis –"

"The slippery bastard." The woman in the cage spat.

"And did threaten to strike him across the head unless he pay you the sum of three shillings and six pence."

"No I never!" She turned to the bailiff. "I asked 'im for one an' six, if you please."

"It has been ordered by the Court of Common Pleas," continued the man, "that, as you refuse to pay the fine of two shillings, you are to be detained on a charge of misconduct and are to remain in the Cage for a period of three days."

The crowd cheered.

"Oh, sod off you bunch of sour farts." The woman made a obscene gesture at the gathering. "And you!" She pointed to a man wearing a flamboyant hairpiece at the back of the crowd.

All heads turned.

"You can forget our little rendez-vous next Friday, Monseur Asseyez mon Face!"

The crowd roared with laughter.

It was then that the first item was thrown. The over-ripe tomato fruit hit the bars of the cage and sent a splatter of red down the front of the captive's chemise. Accompanied with a stream of abuse, the woman picked up what remained of the fruit and hurled it back into the crowd.

Toby decided it was time to leave. He headed down the lane alongside the Turtle Market and back to town. He studied the buildings on each side of Lime Street and wished he had asked the sergeant where the House of Madam Leticia was located. However, at the time, he felt any further inquiries would not have been treated favourably. Once he reached the end of the road he continued his search into High Street; a wide thoroughfare of austere warehouses standing shoulder to shoulder with simply constructed shops and some of the best architecture in the colonies. Some of the houses here were built of brick and stood two or more floors above their neighbours. Toby stood across the street and watched the servants from one of these grand houses: dark-skinned Cameroons transporting heavy goods from an adjacent warehouse.

In preparation for his voyage to Barbados there had been many stories of how the Caribbean islands were now completely populated by Negroes shipped from the continent of Africa to work as slaves on the sugar plantations; stories of how these Negroes had to be whipped until close to death every day in order to prevent them from turning against their English masters. As he watched these servants at their business in the street, Toby could see little evidence of this deplorable treatment. He also observed, contrary to what he had been told, that there were very few Negroes in the town compared to the many other nationalities parading the streets. Social background here was as diverse as nationality: those of high status parading through the streets in their lavish attire made no attempt to disguise their wealth and it was at this time of day that the extravagantly attired mistresses of these houses ventured out for their late afternoon stroll through the town.

Outside the window of a goldsmith, two such ladies stood perusing the rings and pearl necklaces on display. Each held a parasol to keep the last rays of sun from touching the pale skin of their exposed shoulders. It was difficult to assess their age but, by their manner and dress, the two women were probably mistresses at one of the merchant's houses he had seen near the Governor's Mansion. Toby moved to the window in an attempt to catch their conversation.

"You must tell him…" said the older of the two.

"But what if he does not?" whispered the other.

"If he refuse to pay you what is rightfully yours, you tell him he will be hearing from me." The older of the two looked towards Toby askance and they moved away.

The goldsmith's shop made a corner with a quiet side street. Toby took this turning which turned him away from the hustle of the thoroughfare. About half way along this little lane was a building, much larger than the others. Built much in the English style, its upper rooms, supported by a row of oak pillars, projected out over the doorway and into the street. A sign was displayed above the door: *The King's Rose – Punch House of Delights*. Toby tried to get a glimpse through the glass leaded windows but it was too dark to see inside. The house was obviously deserted and there was a notice nailed to the door:

'Madam Leticia welcomes all Gentlemen (and Ladies) in the Pursuit of
Divers Pleasures and Adventure – Open between the hours of sunset and dawn'

At last! Madame Leticia's residence. With the best part of an hour before sunset, Toby decided to visit a church he had passed earlier.

The cemetery overlooked the Caribbean to the south and, although littered with debris from a recent storm, the light air was a refreshing contrast to the stinking thoroughfares in the town. With a renewed optimism, he lifted a cloak of seaweed from the first stone. He may have been greeted with an indecipherable inscription and a malodour of rotting eggs, but he was not to be deterred. He moved eagerly on to the next. However, Toby's enthusiasm was not to last. After inspecting all the gravestones, he slumped on the sea wall. Only one headstone had been inscribed with the name Hopkins, and that was a John Hopkins 1615-1669: Toby's father was born in 1625.

Could the story Jack Bride had told him be true? The old pirate's tales did seem somewhat fanciful. The bloody accounts of the raids on Portabello and the treasure taken were probably exaggerated. But how could Bride know his father's age? And what of his malformed ear? How would Bride be able to guess that? His father hadn't mentioned ever coming to Jamaica; all the letters he wrote had been sent from Virginia. And when Toby made enquiries at the militia office in that colony, they had been about as helpful as the one here at Fort Charles. All they could tell him was that Captain Edward James Hopkins was stationed in Virginia between the years 1660 and 1662 and from there he had been sent to Barbados. And yet the desk sergeant at the fort here hadn't said anything about Barbados: he just confirmed that his father had been here between 1662 and 1667: no records after that date. So what had happened to him since then?

The search for his father had begun when he was seventeen, just eighteen months after the fire that swept through the city of London and took away his mother and sisters. His original purpose for making a new life in the colonies now seemed so far away. Since his arrival in Maryland, Toby had found a new quest, a venture that helped to take away the longing which had been tearing him apart. During those first years in a strange land Toby had discovered in himself a talent for trading: a gift to which he devoted every waking hour. From small beginnings with his little ketch, the *Saint Mary's Fortune*, he made a business connection between the Plymouth Colony and his new home, eventually becoming the owner of a brigantine and an employer of a regular crew of twenty-two hands. And at the age of twenty-five Toby was well on the way to achieving his dream: to establish a commerce between all the colonies in the New World.

Gentle waves broke onto the sand a few paces from the wall where Toby sat; each receding to meet the next, a wash of crystal-clear water attempting to reclaim the town. Beyond the breaking waves the water was smooth, soft; a gentle undulation of sea which reflected the colours of the evening light. A few feet from the waterline, where the little waves began to take shape, a frenzy of activity was about. Several large fish, similar in size and shape to the English river pike, had ventured close to the shore and appeared to be involved in a play of chase. Just a little further down the shore more dorsal fins broke the surface to partake in the game.

Further down the beach a riotous noise caught his attention. A flock of sea birds, similar to the ones which had greeted their vessel when they arrived, were racing up and down the sand as if chasing invisible prey. Toby followed the shoreline to the west. Beyond the promontory where the fort guarded the entrance to the harbour, a three-masted ship had appeared. As soon as it was clear of the point, the vessel changed its heading eastwards. It passed so close to the shore that every command aboard could be heard from the cemetery wall. At the order to furl the mizzen topsail, Toby shook his head. In a light south-westerly such as this, the action would be pointless: surely it would have been better to set a top gallant? He wondered where the ship was heading. If bound for the northern colonies, he hoped she would not fall into the hands of those sea robbers from Tortuga. He looked out across the vast ocean; to the south where the sky meets the sea, to the place where all he had worked for over the years lay at the bottom of its watery grave.

The Chesapeake Venture had been everything to Toby. Seven years it had taken before he could afford a vessel large enough to trade with all the colonies. The brig had been completed four months ago, and this was to be her maiden voyage: Plymouth, Saint Mary, James Town and eventually the Island of Barbados. But like everything in Toby's life, God had decided to take it away. And now, by a twist of fate, he had been brought to the resting place of his father. Toby could feel it inside, could sense it in his heart: as soon as he sat to rest on this sea wall he knew that his father, the only remaining member of his family, was now dead.

The noise from the seabirds was becoming a distraction. His eye caught a movement in the sand not two yards from where he sat. At first he thought it might be a crab searching for morsels brought in with the tide, but once its head appeared he could see it was a newly-hatched sea turtle. So that was what the commotion was about. The heinous birds were taking advantage of a free offering. As soon as the hatchling, a little creature of not more than three inches in length, emerged from its hiding place it scuttled across the dry sand towards the welcoming waves. Should one of the birds see it, Toby prepared himself to leap to its defence. However, there was no need – the baby turtle made it to the sea and swam off to join its brothers.

The determination of this creature was an inspiration. The little fellow had a plan, it followed it through and, against all odds, made it to safety. This is what Toby should be doing. Deliberation was his foe. After all, what could be achieved by just sitting on this wall? He had to set his mind to his task; to find a ship and get his crew back home.

There were several ship-fitters along Queen Street. At the third was advertised for sale a Dutch Fluyt of two hundred and forty tonnes. Toby stepped inside to enquire. The vessel at that time was moored at the harbour waiting to be careened. Although the price was somewhat more than Toby could afford, his Mate had indicated on numerous occasions that he would be interested in making an investment. Toby made an appointment to view the Fluyt that Friday afternoon.

The light was beginning to fade rapidly, yet, despite this, he decided he should look at this craft before returning to his lodgings. A narrow cut connected Queen Street with the harbour and it was along this passage that an unexpected event occurred.

The older of the two ladies he had seen outside the jeweller earlier that afternoon was ambling along this passage towards him. He estimated the woman to be around thirty years of age and seeing her at close quarters, was taken by her classic looks. He stepped aside to allow the lady to pass, taking the opportunity to steal a glance at her narrow waist and delicate bosom.

As is the custom in fashionable society, the woman gave a slight curtsy. To his surprise she also turned to address him.

"May I ask of you one question?"

"Of course." Toby gave a slight bow. He could not help but notice the smooth skin of her shoulders.

"Have you perchance been sent to spy on me?" she asked.

Toby was taken aback by the reproachful look she gave him. "Forgive me, but I do not understand?"

"Was it not you who was standing outside the jewellers in Lime Street earlier today?" she persisted.

"Well, yes I was, but… forgive me, I meant no harm. I have arrived in Port Royal only today and I was about to ask directions to. . ." Toby couldn't very well disclose his search for the house of Madame Leticia.

"To where, may I ask?" The woman's temperament had changed. No longer reproachful, Toby was sure she was now teasing him.

"Well, it is not important," said Toby. "I have since discovered where the place is located."

She looked him up and down. Toby wished he had been better attired. He should have taken the opportunity to purchase some new vestments while in the town.

They were interrupted by a raucous noise from a group who had turned into the alley and were heading in their direction.

"Would you do me a great favour?" The lady gave him a smile. Her eyes, alive and intelligent, were of the palest blue.

"If I am able." Toby was flattered, also relieved to move away from the subject of his search.

"This is not the best part of town for females to venture unattended. Would you do me the honour of escorting me as far as the end of this passage?"

"I would be delighted."

In the meantime the rowdy group had obviously changed their minds and moved back amongst the crowds of Queen Street. However, Toby still thought it wise to accompany the lady, in case they should return.

When they reached the end of the lane, the young woman thanked Toby for his kind deed.

"Tell me," she said cocking her head to one side. "You say you are new to this town?"

"I am."

"Then, should we meet again, I would be honoured to show my gratitude for your gallantry."

With that, the lady curtsied and continued on her way. Toby was convinced that her gestures were somewhat flirtatious. But then, he had been at sea and without female company for several weeks.

The boat was fairly easy to spot, more by its diminutive size than its grandeur: possibly the smallest vessel moored out in the bay. Dwarfed between a four-masted barque and a schooner, the little fluyt gave an impression of a local fishing boat rather than an ocean going vessel. Like a duck rummaging through the weed at the bottom of the pond, the stern rose high out of the water with the gunwale dipping almost to the waterline amidships. She had three masts; the fore and main each bearing two spars, suggesting the vessel could be set with four square sails. However, the mizzen was very short – little more than the length of the bowsprit which, as far as Toby could make out, would only support a fore and aft rig. The promise that this vessel could reach a speed of ten knots seemed very unlikely: more like five when fully loaded. The light was now fading. Moored so far from the shore, it was difficult to ascertain whether the boat was worth the price advertised. He thought it best to wait until he could take a closer look before making any decision.

It was already dark when he returned to his lodgings at the Merchant's Inn. The same four men were playing cards at the oak table in the hall. All went silent as Toby began his ascent up the winding stairs. There was something at odds. His suspicions were further aroused as he reached the top floor: the door of his attic room was half open. Toby drew his pistol and pushed the door with his foot. The room was a mess: the bed cover had been thrown to the floor and the boards pulled away from the wall. All that was left of his clothing was a pair of worn stockings and a kerchief.

Toby descended the stairs two at a time. The proprietor, who had been watching the card game when he arrived, was no longer there. Toby asked of the man's whereabouts, but the group at the table could not account for him – the man had mysteriously vanished.

There was little Toby could do. Notwithstanding, the situation could have been worse. At least he had the foresight to secure his valuables at a financial house, otherwise, he would certainly have lost everything.

Time was moving on. He stepped out into the road and headed back to Lime Street. If he was to get any further with his search, he would need to call in at Madam Leticia's before it got too late.

Chapter 6 – The King's Rose

The King's Rose was a moderately large hall which reminded Toby of his uncle's house in Somerset, although somewhat meagrely furnished with a number of benches and tables of various sizes on a floor of wooden boards. The house was well attended when Toby arrived; a party of gentlemen seated at one of the larger tables and various couples at smaller tables around the perimeter of the hall. The air was infused with the pungent aroma of pipe tobacco. Toby took a place in the far corner where he could observe the activities without being too conspicuous.

The ladies employed by the house were exceptionally well attired considering the nature of their work. Serving wenches busied themselves by ensuring all cups in the house were filled, while those who accompanied gentlemen at the tables appeared to have two objectives; firstly, to encourage their companions to consume as much beverage as their purses could afford, and secondly, to offer their guests an incentive to remain on the premises until their purses were emptied. In Toby's opinion, they were nothing but whores; common strumpets who were bent on draining a man of his honest wealth and of robbing him of any propriety he may otherwise hold dear.

It appeared that while most of the party seated at the centre table were respectful of the females in their company, some in the group were overtly familiar; one gentleman taking the liberty of kissing the neck of his companion while his hands stroked her bosom, another having a wench sit on his lap just so he could venture his hand under her petticoats. This public display did not seem to deter the girls in any way; in fact they appeared to encourage it. Even the proprietor showed little concern at such behaviour. A woman of ample proportions, Madam Leticia roamed the house like a matriarch giving her orders to the serving girls while attending her clientèle. Toby shrank as she approached his table. When asked if he would like the company of one of her girls, he declined. However, no sooner had she moved away, he felt conspicuous sitting alone at his table and wished he had accepted her invitation.

What had he hoped to achieve by coming here? The sergeant at the military office had suggested that he might gain information as to the whereabouts of his father, but what was the chance of that? He imagined the room falling silent should he inquire if anyone had seen his father. Surely the house would collapse with laughter!

He was about to leave when a young woman at the far side of the room caught his eye. Toby didn't recognise her at first, however, as she approached his table, he recalled the coquettish smile.

"Well. How charmed that we meet again, and so soon!" she said. "I had not expected to see you here."

She was exceptionally well dressed; a beautiful scarlet bodice with a long narrow waistline, a full skirt, embroidered with gold thread opened at the front to reveal an elaborately trimmed petticoat in gold satin.

"I must say that I am the one who is charmed," Toby replied. "It was a mistake, my coming here. I was about to leave."

The woman pulled up a chair and sat down beside him. She leaned across the table and took a deep breath revealing much of the soft flesh above the cut of her bodice. "That would be such misfortune, I was hoping we could become better acquainted." she said.

"Oh no, I am in no great hurry to go." It was a fact that Toby was relieved to see a familiar face.

"My name is Elizabeth." The young woman held out her hand to be kissed.

"Oh yes, forgive me." He took her hand gently and brushed her fingers with his dry lips. "Tobias. . . er, Toby Hopkins." He released her hand as if it were a hot iron. "I should explain. . . I was dispirited, feeling a little out of place in here. But now that –"

"Would you like me to stay with you?" she said.

"Well yes, of course. I was about to ask you –"

"Then you must purchase a drink while I sit with you." The woman's tone had changed; her manner was now quite abrupt.

"Forgive me. Of course," Toby turned to look about the room. "I shall call for. . ." his words trailed off as a serving girl was already at their table. Toby was about to hold up his cup but Elizabeth took it from his hand and peered over the brim.

"Rum-punch. Kill-Devil," she grimaced. "Toby, this is poison. Make a habit of drinking this and it will very soon burn your insides." She placed the cup disdainfully at the end of the table and spoke to the girl. "Two French brandies, Sally."

While the price was high, Toby found the brandy to be far more palatable than the drink handed to him on his arrival. They were silent for a moment, then he remembered their encounter earlier that day.

"I pray you reached your destination without incident this evening?" he said, hoping this would remind his companion of his gallant act.

Elizabeth leant forward to take up her cup, the soft light of the room reflecting the delightful shape of her neck and the gentle curve of her breast. She leaned back against the wall.

"Do you like me?" she said.

"Well, yes. It is refreshing to find such pleasing company."

"Why did you come here?" Her tone; once again, abrupt.

"Oh yes, I almost forgot. I came to seek news of my father."

"It does not disturb you to find your father in a house such as this?"

"I do not expect to find him here. No, I have come here to enquire as to his whereabouts. I have not seen him since he left my home in England when I was ten years old."

"And you believe he is here, in Port Royal?"

"It seems he was, yes."

"What is his name?"

"Edward Hopkins. He was stationed here as a captain in the militia."

Elizabeth called the proprietor over to listen to Toby's story. With his approval she added that there would be a small reward for any useful information. Madam Leticia promised to do everything in her powers to help with such a worthy cause and Toby repeated what he had told Elizabeth. Little did he realise that this action would change the course of his life.

The proprietor spoke to the mulatto youth who had been cavorting with the party at the long table. Toby watched the boy as he wandered around the room conversing with some of the customers.

"Does that boy take your fancy? I could introduce him if it pleases you."

Shocked at such a suggestion, Toby quickly turned away. "Oh, no! You have me wrong, I have no inclination . . . What I mean to say is –"

"I shall ask you again, Toby. And after this, I shall pursue this matter no further." She waited until he had her full attention. "Do you wish my company?"

"Of course, it gives me great pleasure to be with you."

Elizabeth leaned back and smiled. "Well, thank you."

At once her frivolous manner resumed, and from then on Toby was much at ease in the company of this beautiful young woman. Having had the privilege of an education, he was familiar with the ways of conversing with society ladies which meant he and Elizabeth were able to discuss many things together; his childhood days in London, his indenture in Maryland, his recent adventures with the buccaneers.

"What are your plans for the future? Do you intend to continue trading?" she asked.

"At this moment I am without a vessel but, yes, once I have procured one I plan to start over again."

"That is very commendable of you, Toby. Many people would be discouraged after experiencing the misadventures you have been through."

Unused as he was to such compliments, Toby flushed.

"Have you considered setting up trade between Jamaica and the colonies in the north?" she said.

"Not as yet. My main concern now is to return my crew to their homes."

"I am sure. However, it may be worth considering for the future."

Toby looked around the hall. Would these gentlemen be the sort he would be prepared to trade with? He thought not. "I have no contacts here in Port Royal."

"Then if you . . . " Elizabeth took a sip of her brandy.

Toby waited until she replaced the glass on the table. "You were about to say?"

"What? Oh yes. It was of no importance. Tell me what is your impression of Port Royal?"

The conversation flowed along in a light course, and Toby was enamoured with such convivial company. However, something was lacking; a flaw in his approach to the etiquette of verbal intercourse: Toby had failed to show any interest in the affairs of his companion. While this flaw in his character may have been slight, it did not escape the attention of Elizabeth, who took great interest in the affairs of Tobias Hopkins. The conversation continued in this manner until they were interrupted. A brown-skinned girl of about twenty years of age and dressed in the attire of a house-maid was standing at their table.

"Beatrice!" exclaimed Elizabeth.

Ignoring the remark, the girl had her eyes fixed on Toby.

"You the one who want to know about Captain Hopkins?"

"Yes, I am," Toby replied. "Do you know something?"

"Maybe that I do," The girl pulled up a chair and sat beside him.

Toby turned to call for a drink but the serving wench was already there. All three women considered the weight of Toby's purse as he took out and broke into a silver eight-real coin. He waited until the wench was gone, then turned to their new companion.

"Can you tell me what you know?"

"The captain know my Aunt," she replied.

Elizabeth, who had been excluded from the conversation thus far, leaned across the table. "Why have you not come to see me?" she whispered to the girl.

"You not send for me no more."

"Your Aunt?" Toby tried to regain the girl's attention. "Is she here now?"

"But did you not get my message?" Elizabeth demanded.

"She have a farm in Saint Andrew, up in the hills." The girl turned to Elizabeth. "What message? I get no message!"

Elizabeth raised her eyes to the heavens. "Three weeks ago, I gave a note for Lucian to pass to you. Did you not read it?"

Beatrice drummed her fingers on the table. "How can I read it when I not get it?"

Toby intervened. "Is it possible that I could arrange to meet your Aunt?" he asked.

"Possible, maybe," she turned back to Elizabeth. "What the note say?"

Toby was both frustrated and confused. He also needed the gentleman's room. Having observed the occasional person pass through the door at the end of the hall, he excused himself from the table.

The mulatto boy had positioned himself at the door for the purpose of procuring a fee for use of the facility. Toby was relieved to be allowed through without further incident.

However, the room which he entered was not for the function he had expected. Within the space of ten by twelve cubits, a collection of tables had been joined together to form a raised platform. A group of gentlemen had assembled in a circle around this stage as if preparing themselves for an entertainment. Once he moved to the front, Toby was able to see the object of their attention. At the centre of the stage stood a wooden chair on which sat a pewter jug. On the back of the chair was thrown a lady's dress.

The owner of the dress was one of the wenches Toby had seen accompanying the party in the main hall earlier that evening. Attired only in her petticoats, the woman strutted around the chair inviting her audience to partake in a play: a game which elicited those who had her attention to toss a coin onto the stage.

The first coin rolled across the platform and landed at the front edge of the stage. With her back to her benefactor, the whore bent down to pick up this offering; an act which was performed in such a manner as to raise her petticoats and reveal to him much of the bare flesh above her stocking. The game was repeated with more eager participants from the audience. Encouraged by her admirers, the wench made a display of adding up the collected coins in her hand and let them drop into the jug. At this point there was a hearty cheer as she, in a provocative and suggestive manner, removed another item of her clothing.

It was during these activities that Toby became aware that he was being watched. Across the far side of the room, with his back against the wall, was someone who twice caught his eye during the show. On each occasion the man looked quickly away as if he did not wish his observations to be discovered. He was fair, clean shaven and quite tall, but most of the time the man was obscured by the audience and it was difficult to ascertain any other feature.

Toby's attention was diverted to another in the crowd; a rough looking youth he had noticed leaning against the door when he first entered the room. The ruffian had made his way through the crowd and now stood close to the portly gentleman who had just thrown a coin onto the stage. At the moment the wench bent to collect her prize, the youth slipped his hand under the gentleman's belt and extracted his purse. The movement had been delivered with such stealth and speed that, had Toby not been paying close attention, he would certainly have missed the action altogether.

No sooner had the deed been committed; the young rascal disappeared from view. Toby searched all the faces in the crowd – not a sign of the boy. Nor could he see the fair-haired man who had been spying on him. He could only presume they had both left before the entertainment was over.

Toby had entered this room under false pretences. Yet, despite his moral predicament, he remained until the final act of the play was over: until the wench, naked and shameless, departed with great applause from the company.

It was whilst milling with the returning crowd Toby had a glimpse of the young pick-pocket again; his long dark coat almost brushing the floor as he headed for the door to the street. Following him, three paces behind, was the tall fair-haired man who had been observing Toby.

It was with a certain trepidation that Toby returned to his table. While he did his best to conceal himself amid the crowd, he could not avoid being observed by his two female companions who were now sitting close together awaiting his return. They said nothing as he pulled up a chair.

"I hope you will forgive my absence, but –"

"Methinks our master has discovered an entertainment more worthy than our company?" Elizabeth looked to her brown-eyed companion. "Do you not think so, my sweet?"

Both girls broke into unrestrained laughter.

"I can only apologise," Toby continued. "My excuse is that I was waylaid."

This only worsened the situation. Both girls were now shaking in their attempt at restraint. Toby could feel the blood rise to his cheeks.

Elizabeth placed her arm around Beatrice's waist and pressed a finger to her lips. She looked at Toby. "Do you imagine that we are incapable of entertaining ourselves in your absence?"

Seeing the hurt in Toby's eyes, Beatrice reached out and took his hand. "We play with you. You not see that?" she placated. "It not that we want to be unkind."

"We have been discussing the matter of your lodgings," Elizabeth said. "We both believe that it would be unsafe for you to return to that place in York Street."

Toby was relieved at this new turn in the conversation. "I have to agree with you," he said, releasing himself from Beatrice's hand and raising his cup. "However, I am a little perplexed to know what to do."

"We may have the solution," Elizabeth continued. "We have taken the liberty of asking the proprietor of this place if she could accommodate you. And, as fortune would have it, she has a room available." Elizabeth held up her hand before Toby could object. "The room is particularly well-appointed and normally reserved for Lord Rumsay, who now happens to be in England."

"I'm not so sure." Toby was not one to accept proposals lightly.

"He not even goin' to look?" Beatrice made no attempt to hide her disbelief.

"Well, if you think it would be suitable," Toby sighed, "I have no alternative."

At this point they were interrupted by a disturbance at the entrance. An unruly group led by a large fashionably dressed gentleman who, by the way he carried himself had clearly been drinking to excess, entered the room and made a fuss about being accommodated at a table. The proprietor, rather than dismissing the group, arranged that a table be brought in from the annex and set up in the centre of the room.

Toby was curious to know who the gentleman was to be given so much attention.

"That is Henry Morgan. The man who has been appointed deputy-governor of this island." Elizabeth gave the group a disapproving look. "And what a mistake that was."

Toby tried to recall where he'd heard that name. "I am sure I have encountered him before."

"He an evil man," Beatrice sucked through her teeth. "You not want to mix with he."

Then Toby recalled Jack Bride's story. "Now I remember. He had some connection with my father."

Before his enthusiasm got the better of him, Elizabeth touched Toby's arm and suggested they move to Lord Rumsay's rooms. She caught the attention of Madam Leticia.

Outside the windows of the hall of Madame Leticia's residence the moon was high and the street was bathed in a cool light. Not fifty yards away, the youth who had minutes before left the King's

Rose, was relieving himself against the wall of the first building in an alley. Across the other side of the street, under the shadows of a gable, two men were keeping a close watch on the young ruffian. One of his observers was fair and about six feet tall, the other was a few inches shorter and as skinny as a fishing pole.

The skinny one took a step forward.

The fair one pulled him back into the shadows. "Wait! Not yet. Too many people here. Are you sure the purse he took is belonging to the one we want?"

"Yes, the fat man. I seen him."

"The same one who is visiting at the Colonel's house in Spanish Town?"

"He were there at least three times in the last two weeks, Mister G. I seen him with me own eyes."

They waited as a couple stepped out from the doorway three houses down the alley. Taking care to avoid the stream which crossed their path, they commented their disapproval to the youth who then responded with an obscene gesture. The couple moved on towards the main street.

"And there was definitely no-one else in the house?" the fair man persisted.

"I checked, you seen me. Anyways, we both seen the girl leave before midnight – just like she always do."

"You should have finished off the dog. Then we could have been looking in the room."

The youth, who had now finished his ablutions, followed the couple down the street and resumed his obscenities. It was not until the man raised his fist did the boy leave them. With his long coat swinging, he took a left turn into Prince Street.

The two men waited until the youth had turned the corner before they stepped out of the shadows. They followed at a discreet distance until the boy moved into Brick Lane; a secluded street which ran along the back of the meat market. Here, they quickened their pace and eventually caught up with him outside the doors of a salt-packing house.

"Hold up there, cousin!"

The boy turned to face the barrel of a pistol.

The skinny one, face as pale as a wraith under the still moonlight, moved close. "Don't you try nothing or you'll not see the sun rise on the morrow."

"What do you want? I ain't done nothing to you!"

The man with the pistol moved forward, his voice as cool as a judge. "All we are wanting is that purse you took from the fat gentleman at Leticia's place."

"What purse? I ain't –"

The skinny man, with the wiry strength of a simian, took the youth's arm and twisted it behind his back. The boy sank to his knees and let out an unearthly howl.

The pistol pressed against the youth's head. "We do not wish to hurt you. All we are wanting is the purse. And then we let you go."

The boy's arm was pulled further up his back, the pistol pushed against his cheek.

"I'll give it, I'll give it!" he screamed. Reaching inside his coat, the boy tossed a small bag into the road.

The fair one crossed the street. The purse was made of pigskin; soft to the touch, and light too. He picked it up as a commotion started up. The skinny one was standing over the boy; cudgel raised high above his head.

Eyes wide with terror, the youth pleaded to the man who was inspecting the contents of the purse. The first blow struck with a dull thud, sending him scuttling across the dirt like a sand crab. He tried to protect himself, but it was hopeless. His attacker was relentless. It was as if he had been taken over by a demon. Blow after blow he struck, and continued to strike long after the youth was dead. When the tirade was over, the skinny one, exhausted, slumped down to rest against the door of the salt-house. Less than five feet away the youth lay motionless in the street.

The fair one ambled over to squat down between them. "Was that necessary? You really must be knowing when to stop." He emptied the purse into the dust; three silver coins, an iron key and a little silver Star of David. "Now this is what I want you to do," he said, slipping the key into his pocket. "You will collect Pierre and meet me at the side entrance of the jeweller's in New Street in one hour." He stood up. "You know where this is?"

Still slumped against the salt-house door, the skinny one nodded. He took a deep breath and knelt in the road. "Do we have to bring the Frenchman?"

The fair man stood over and watched him scratch through the dust for the remaining items of the purse. "Why should we not bring him?"

"What I mean is, Mister G, don't you think he be a bit strange? Like he takes some pleasure from it all?"

The fair one gave him a cold look. "At least he is not messing up like you did last night." He looked toward the figure lying in the gutter. Blood as dark as molasses spilled from the side of the youth's head and soaked into the salt crystals that littered the road. "And I am thinking this is no better." He shook his head and turned to go. "One hour then. Yes?"

Without looking up, the skinny man nodded. He was entranced; fascinated by the way the cool moonlight bounced off the little silver hexagram in his hand.

Chapter 7 – **Diverse Pleasures**

Elizabeth had visited Lord Rumsay's rooms at The King's Rose on many occasions. The accommodation was as it always was; an oak dining table with six covered chairs, a *lit a repose* sofa, a hand-crafted dresser in the modern French style and a very ample four-poster bed with hangings embroidered with crewel wool. The well proportioned glass window was furnished with a beautifully woven hanging which depicted a forest scene with all kind of birds and beasts. The room would not have been out of place at the new palace of the King of France.

While the rent was twice that of his room in York Street, their companion seemed impressed and suggested that she and Beatrice adjust themselves while he excused himself to settle the account with Madam Leticia.

During his absence the two women, in playful mood, discovered a closet filled with ladies attire and various bottles of scent. At Elizabeth's suggestion, and with great haste, Beatrice threw off her uniform and changed into a gown to suit the occasion.

Their new friend had generously ordered a meal for himself and his two guests which was brought up by one of the serving waitresses from the hall. Before she left, Elizabeth handed the girl a note.

"Give this to Carlo and ask him to deliver it to Beatrice's aunt at La Bruma. He will know where. Thank you Mary."

After the girl had left, Elizabeth lit two candles and arranged the table; generous slices of cured ham, a platter of fruit, some bread and a jug of wine. The two women then positioned themselves at each side of the head of the table, reserving a place between them for their companion.

It was apparent, during their earlier conversation, that Elizabeth had much in common with Toby. A pity he had been reluctant to ask about her past. For had he done so, he would have discovered they had some similarities; an upbringing in the city, a classical education and an interest in the arts. However, her reasons for coming out to the colonies were not the same as he. Elizabeth had been enticed into an early marriage to a man with favourable prospects; a husband who later turned out to be a philanderer who had deserted her six years since. With little left of her dowry and much preferring the life of an independent woman in Jamaica, Elizabeth had no desire to return to her previous life in England. Toby, on the other hand, had a past clouded in mystery. While he had been willing to tell about his search for his estranged father, he was less than forthcoming when asked about the family he left behind. While she detected a certain reserve in Toby's advances towards her, he did seem to be at ease in the company of Beatrice. He was obviously taken by her innocent charm and looks; attributes which Elizabeth also admired. It was by fortune that this chance meeting with Tobias Hopkins had brought Beatrice back to her, and it would be by design that Elizabeth intended to reclaim her.

"What do you make of him?" she asked.

"He fine."

"I know he is arrogant, as are all men. But he is also sensitive, which I think is charming. Do you not think him interesting?"

Beatrice pursed her lips. "He not say much."

"Well, he may be somewhat restrained in our company but I believe we could help him to be more comfortable." She took her friend's hand. "I have an idea. But first, you must tell me. Does he take your fancy?"

"Yes, I like him. But I think he not like me."

"You are mistaken, I am sure of it." Elizabeth squeezed her hand. "The man needs a little encouragement."

"How we goin' do that?"

Elizabeth studied her friend. At last she was showing some interest. She leaned across and tucked the strap of Beatrice's bodice beneath her gown. The touch of her soft skin reminded her of past adventures they had shared. "Did you miss my company while we were apart?"

"You want that I show you?" Beatrice got up from her chair and moved around the table. She bent down and kissed her; gentle at first, but then more passionate, as if the passing of time had charged her embrace. Had it not been for the sound of footsteps outside, who knows where the kiss may have led? Beatrice quickly returned to her chair.

Elizabeth whispered across the table. "I think we should show him how we feel for each other. We should encourage him."

Toby seemed to be in good spirits when he returned to his newly acquired accommodation. Elizabeth was watchful as she poured each of them a glass of wine and they settled down to eat. The food was palatable and the conversation flowed as smoothly as the wine. She noticed that Toby was particularly attentive to Beatrice during the meal.

"Have you always lived here?" he asked.

"Port Royal?"

"Jamaica."

"I born in Santa Augusta, in Clarendon Parish."

"Do your family still reside there now?"

"My father, he in Cuba. He take one of me brother."

"Do you see them?"

"I never seen my father. He leave before I born. He Spanish, go when the English come."

Toby's expression was thoughtful, calculating.

"Do you have any others in your family?"

"Two brothers an' a sister" the girl hesitated, "that all."

"So they live in Clarendon?"

"Aye, aye, aye, you ask so much!" Beatrice exclaimed.

Toby flushed. "Please forgive me. It is only that I am interested in your life here. I should not be so –"

"No, no. It good." Beatrice gave him an encouraging smile. "I not mind. You want hear?"

"If it does not trouble you so."

Elizabeth, amused by Toby's interest in her friend, topped up their glasses and sat back to listen to Beatrice's account of her past. She looked wonderful that evening; as if she had always belonged to these opulent surroundings. And that gown suited her perfectly. Such a narrow waist: no need to be fussing with corsets and stays. She was lucky to inherit her father's hair too; long shiny ringlets cascading onto her soft shoulders: none of the tight curls other mulatto women had to endure.

"Me Mama belong to Senor Miguel Consavez," Beatrice continued. "He have big house in Esperanza. She give him four childs – two girl an' two boy."

Elizabeth loved to listen to Beatrice talk: her eyes, as dark as the night sparkling in the candlelight with every animated turn. And her mouth; full and sensuous, glistening with every word. Beatrice was often short on words, but when they did flow, her expressions were a delight to watch.

"So when the English come to Jamaica, the Spanish free many slaves so to help them fight. Some go, some stay. Me big brother go to the hills in the north – I never seen him. Mama has me in her belly so she keep me an' me sister an' we live in Clarendon." Beatrice paused. "You want know all this?"

Toby nodded.

"So then she live with a free man, him called Emanuelo, and we all live on farm near Santa Augusta. When I is sixteen Mama move to St Jago an' I come to Port Royal to work."

"For Madam Leticia?"

"For two year in this house, then housemaid for merchant man in town. I work there now." Beatrice chuckled at Toby's confused expression. "You want ask me more?"

"How did your aunt acquire the farm?" asked Toby.

Beatrice looked across at Elizabeth. "It not her farm. She –"

"So, dear Toby," Elizabeth intervened. "Now that we are better acquainted, why don't you enlighten us with some of your own past?"

Toby shifted uneasily in his chair. "But have I not done so already? Surely you have heard enough of my story."

"On the contrary, I am intrigued to learn of your family. Did you not say you lived in London? That must have been a great change for you to come over here."

"Oh there is little to say. I came to Mary-Land to forget about my past."

"That has me even more curious." There was a mischievous sparkle in Elizabeth's eyes. "Were you a notorious highwayman eluding the gallows?" she teased.

"Oh, no! Nothing as exciting."

"How about a philanderer then, running from your bride with her dowry?"

Elizabeth avoided Beatrice's look.

There was a moment or two of silence around the table, each with their own thoughts.

"Do you have a sweetheart back in Mary-Land?" Elizabeth asked.

"I have a friend in the Plymouth Colony, Sarah. We sailed across from England together."

"Just the two of you?"

"She was accompanied by her family."

"So you have known each other for some time. Are you promised to each other?"

Toby took a sip from his glass. "Well no, but we are very close."

Elizabeth cupped her hands under her chin. "Plymouth. Is that not the settlement of the Puritans?"

"Some call them that," Toby replied defensively.

"Then it must be difficult for the two of you to be alone together – considering their strict rules," she mused.

"We are free to see each other whenever I visit the colony." He turned to Beatrice. "Can you tell me about your aunt?"

Beatrice, who had her glass poised to her mouth, placed it back on the table. "She live in –"

"Enough of this banter," Elizabeth brushed the crumbs of bread from a plate. "Let us play a game." She picked two grapes from the bowl and placed them in the centre of the plate.

"The last to take a grape will make a choice," she said. "They may either, drink a full glass of wine in one taking, or dance one round of the Sarabande with the partner of their choosing."

"Sarabande?" Beatrice looked confused.

"You will know it, my sweet. You have seen it many times at your master's house."

"If you say," Beatrice pursed her lips.

"There is one rule," Elizabeth continued. "The grape must be taken without the aid of hands." She studied the two faces at the table. "Do we all agree?"

Both Toby and Beatrice shrugged. They were in collusion; resigned to fall in with her plan.

"So," Elizabeth placed her palms on the table, "Hands down… begin!"

At the great oak table in the private rooms of Lord Rumsay three contestants bent forwards and pressed their faces together like hungry dogs. Heads pushed against heads, cheeks caressed cheeks, lips touched mouths: each contestant intent on being the first to take a morsel between their teeth.

As one would expect, Elizabeth, with past experience at this game, was the first to raise her head; a purple grape held lightly betwixt her teeth. She sat back in her chair and studied the tactics of her two companions in their struggle to reach the fruit. Every flick of the tongue, every brush of lips brought a smile to Elizabeth's face. Finally, her dearest friend and accomplice, Beatrice, surfaced triumphantly with the prize clasped between her glistening lips. Toby, cheeks glowing from the rigours of the contest, now had to decide his fate. He straightened up and made the diplomatic choice: to consume the wine. Both girls applauded as their host tilted his head back to drain the last drop from his glass.

Two more grapes were tossed onto the plate. This time it was Beatrice who was the first one to rise; her turn to observe the lithe and graceful moves of her mistress. Anyone could see that Elizabeth was playing a tactical ruse; for whenever Toby caught the little purple fruit between his teeth, Elizabeth would prize it away with the flick of her tongue, and yet, each time she closed her mouth onto the morsel, it unaccountably escaped from her lips. Throughout the contest, if she wasn't occupied with the chase, Elizabeth would constantly seek the mouth of her opponent.

At last Toby rose up, glorious from the scene. The grape firmly grasped between his teeth, he sank back in the chair.

Exhausted after their passionate engagement, Elizabeth rested her head against Toby's shoulder. "Oh well," she sighed. "That was certainly an exciting contest." She raised her legs onto the table. With a discreet signal to Beatrice she got her to remove her shoes and, through half-closed eyes, watched the girl trace her fingers along the gentle curve of her leg. How intoxicated she was by the girl's touch. How so much she wanted her to venture further. And how so much she yearned to touch Beatrice; to run her fingers down her back, to explore the shape below, to reach that beautiful curve which her friend had always tried to conceal.

With her head resting against his chest, Elizabeth could also feel the tension in Toby. While he said nothing, she knew his eyes were fixed on Beatrice; on the gentle rise and fall of her breasts. She also knew he would be powerless to resist the movement of her own hand which now caressed the inside of his thigh. Could she dare to venture a little further; to seek proof of his desire for her dear friend? Lost in the sensuality of it all, the three remained silent, allowing action to take its own course.

But, for Elizabeth, the game was not yet over. She lifted her head from Toby's shoulder, removed her feet from the table and straightened up. "Now. I believe it is my turn to decide my fate," she said. "And for my forfeit, I shall choose to dance. But who shall be my partner, I wonder?" She looked from one to the other. "I choose. . . Toby!"

Taking his hand she led him to the centre of the room. "I trust you are familiar with the Sarabande, Toby."

"I think so. But, if I remember correctly, surely it is a sholo, I mean a solo dance?"

"Then so be it. We shall observe how it is done in the English court." Elizabeth sank into the sofa and signalled for Beatrice to join her. The two young women, already fuelled with desire, sat close together humming a familiar theme while their host attempted the intricate steps of the courtly dance.

So focused was Toby on perfecting the opening moves that he failed to notice the actions of his female companions a few feet away. Shifting his weight to his right leg, he raised the other a few inches and began to shake it to the rhythm of the accompanying trill. The movement caught him off balance and he had to let his foot drop to regain his composure. His audience decided to give Toby another chance and, rather than interrupt the performance, continued their humming unabated. This decision not only suggested that his indiscretion had gone unnoticed, but also allowed the two lustful women time to indulge in their own amusement. Their companion fell in with their scheme and made a second attempt. This time the movement was a success. With a beam of pride, Toby took his eyes from his feet and, looked up towards the *lit a repose*. His jaw dropped. The two women, each with a hand under the other's petticoats, couldn't help but giggle at the sight of their new friend. Poised with one foot aloft and mouth agape, Toby's cheeks were as flushed as his companions. But, in his case, it was not with lust: the poor man was embarrassed. The two ladies stood up and applauded.

While this may have eased the situation, it was now obvious to Elizabeth that Toby would be of little use in the next stage of her scheme. She led him to the sofa and pressed her cheek against his. "Methinks your memory needs refreshing," she whispered.

Toby looked confused.

"Of the steps of the Sarabande. Beatrice and I shall remind you." She moved to her friend. "Would you prefer to dance a Menuet with me, my sweet?" She pronounced the name in the French way.

Beatrice was already poised for the dance and they began to hum a popular tune by Henry Lawes. Toby, his glass waving in the air as if it were Lully's conducting stick, joined in with the refrain while the two girls; arms outstretched, fingers barely touching, danced the graceful steps of the Menuet; each turn, every elegant dip, executed with such grace as if they were performing a ballet de court.

From his reclined position, Toby watched through half-closed eyes as the two dancers glided across the floor. The ballet soon began to take on a more personal form; movements more tactile, more sensual. Their bodies teased; in one moment they came together, in the next they were apart. While the objective of this performance may have been to give encouragement to their companion, the women were lost in their own interpretation and continued to dance long after Toby had lost consciousness.

Chapter 8 – **The Silversmith**

It was at the moment when the two women at the King's Rose were about to begin their interpretation of the Menuet that the silversmith, Mr Aaron Rubens, arrived at his home in New Street a little worse for drink. He leaned against the door and searched his pockets once again for his purse. It was only when the back door swung open he realised that he hadn't mislaid his key after all. All his fears proved to be unfounded: he had obviously forgotten to take it with him.

As was his usual habit, he armed himself with a glass of port and an oil lamp from the kitchen and headed for the stairs. Careful not to make a sound as he passed the room on the first landing, he paused to take a breath before continuing to the upper floor. It wasn't until he reached his own room and placed the glass and lamp on the table beside his bed that he realised that something was amiss. The first thing he noticed were the papers from his desk scattered over the floor. He turned around and steadied himself at the edge of the bed. The chair, which he always positioned next to the window, had been moved to the centre of the room. His jaw dropped, burying his chin into the fleshy folds below. Could this be true? He squeezed his puffy eyes and shook his head. But it was true: this was no apparition. There were definitely three men standing in the shadows of his bed-chamber. All of them strangers and certainly not the kind of gentlemen Aaron Rubens would invite into his home for Hanukkah. The tallest of the three was the first to speak.

"Mister Rubens, come and sit." The man signalled to the chair.

"What in the name of – Who are you?"

A pistol was pushed against Rubens forehead. "Please, do as I ask and you will not be harmed."

"Look, take what you like," pleaded the silversmith. "I can bring you some good quality ware from the shop, if you –"

The man held up his hand. "Sit down! Now, Mister Rubens." He nodded to the one standing by the door who then stepped forwards, took Rubens by his arm and pushed him into the chair.

"Now, I am going to be clear with you." The tall man leaned over him, a thin scar in the shape of the letter G glinted in the lamplight beneath his crop of hair. "We are not interested in your valuables, Mister Rubens. We are only needing to ask you a few questions. And, if you can answer them truthfully, we will leave you in peace. You understand?"

Rubens sat in silence, his eyes still watering from the pain along his right arm.

The third accomplice, a man who had the appearance of a wild ape, was now alongside. The silversmith recoiled at the stench of stale sweat as the man bent forward and ripped open the front of Ruben's shirt. But it was when he took his knife and drew a thin line across his belly that he screamed.

"Yes, yes! Ask what you will!" he pleaded. "But please, tell him to stop."

The tall one nodded and the ape resumed his earlier position on the floor at the far side of the bed.

"Now, the first question I am wanting to ask is, who is Mister Keach?"

And that is how the questioning began.

Over an hour later all three men were still waiting for an answer.

Irritated by the steady clunk from across the far side of the room, Jack pressed his back against the door frame. He did his best to ignore the sound. At least there was now some light and a few objects for him to look at. The candle-holder for a start, with its solid base and seven silver arms: that would fetch quite a lot. Silhouetted against the moonlit street, it was one of the first things Jack noticed when they came in. If only Mister G would let him take it.

The silversmith, his arms tightly clasped together behind his back with neat coils of hemp rope, shifted his corpulent weight in the wooden chair.

Mr G leaned forward. "I am asking you again. Who is Keach?"

The man recoiled. "I already said, I have never encountered that name before."

"Then what was your business with Colonel Brown?"

"Colonel Brown? I don't have much to do with –"

"We saw you visit his house three times in the past two weeks. That is not having much to do with him?" He moved up close to the silversmith. "I think it is, Mister Rubens."

Rubens flinched. He moved his head to one side. "I just collect import duty from the vessels that arrive into the harbour."

"And?"

"I arrange storage for the Governor's share."

His interrogator rubbed a scar at his forehead with the tip of his forefinger.

Clunk!

Jack held his breath and did his best to ignore the figure at the far side of the room. He studied the splatters that covered the toes of his own cowhide boots. He had bought them at the market less than two weeks before and now they were ruined. Even in this dim light the stains were noticeable to anyone.

"Now, I want you to think carefully. Back to the year sixty-eight. What work were you making at this time?"

The fat man frowned.

"Your work?"

"Oh, I was a clerk at the Harbour office."

"More than a clerk, I am thinking. Yes?"

The man didn't reply.

"I believe that you are keeping records of all the crews and musters at this time. Is this not true?"

"I did, but that was more than ten years past. How am I to remember –"

"You remember the raids on the town of Portobello. Yes?

The silversmith nodded.

Clunk!

Jack looked over to the Frenchman. Why he had to stick grenades to his belt he just could not understand. It wasn't as if he was ever going to need them – at least not for this kind of work. It was illegal for a start. The authorities couldn't do nothing about people wearing swords and pistols around town, but there were enough notices posted about banning grenades. Not that anyone would be brave or stupid enough to challenge the French pig: that would be like asking the man to settle his debt or to remove his shoes. It was as if the ape wanted to get noticed. And like Mister G says, the last thing they need is to get attention to themselves now.

Clunk!

He glared at the figure on the floor; back straight as a board, chest all puffed up. Arms straight – up he goes, arms bend – back to the floor, *clunk*! Up – pause – down, *clunk*! For a whole hour they had to put up with this. It was only when the owner turned up that Mr G told the Frenchman to stop. Of course, he had to make a big show of tying the man to the chair: but at least it kept him quiet for a while. And now it started all over again: up – down, *clunk*! Up – down, *clunk*! Why did they have to have him along with them? Last night they were fine without him – well, a bit messy maybe, but at least they got the job done.

Jack looked at his boots again; maybe they'd scrub up in the morning. Dammed if he was going to throw them away. *Clunk!* He gripped the cudgel at his belt – just a few steps. But the chair would be in his way. Would Mister G be able to stop him before he got there?

Clunk!

Mr G looked at Jack then turned towards the Frenchman. "Pierre, you can stop that now." He waited until the man spread his sweaty bulk across the bed before resuming his interrogation.

"And you must be remembering the booty which was missing from the vessel, *Trident*."

Rubens remained silent. His wig had slipped and a bead of sweat escaped down the side of his face. A hand was at his throat; fingers sinking into the soft flesh under his chin. They squeezed.

"Yes, yes, I remember." The fat man spluttered.

The Frenchman, now busying himself with removing the dirt from under his nails, wiped the tip of his knife onto the bed cover and looked up. As far as he was concerned, his work here was as good as finished. All he had left to do was wait for *Le Maitre* to give him the word, then he would finish the fat man off. A shame there was no-one else here to play with; girls were always the best, but a boy would do. Like the one they had two weeks ago – the old sodomite's boyfriend. The man actually pissed himself before he even started on him!

But today will be no fun. He watched *Le Maitre* with the man in the chair.

"Then what about Keach?"

"I promise you, I know nothing about Keach."

"And Cooper? What did he come to see you about?"

The man in the chair seemed to be frightened at the mention of this name.

"Tell me about Cooper, or I'll set this man onto you."

Rubens gave a quick look at the figure lying across his bed. "I didn't meet with Cooper. It was a Captain Hopkins who came to see me. He wanted us to see Cooper together, but nothing ever happened."

"Why did Hopkins want this meeting?"

"I don't know. He didn't say."

Jack was standing by the door, shifting his feet like a scurry-rat. He stopped as soon as *Le Maitre* straightened up and walked towards him.

"When we were at Leticia's this evening there was a man who is asking about Hopkins. Do you remember him?"

"The one sittin' at the table with the two strumpets?"

"The same, yes. When we are finishing here I want you to watch him. Yes?"

"Shall I ask around?"

"No, just see what he is doing. But let me know if he is making his way to the Hopkins' farm."

"The farm in St Andrew? Where the Negro woman lives?"

"Yes, that farm."

"Will do, Mister G."

"Now, I am thinking we will be here for a long time. While I am getting this man to talk, I want you to look in the other rooms in this house to seeing what you can find. You can do this?"

"Yes, Mister G."

Jack slipped into the hall and Mr G returned to his position at the foot of the bed.

"There was a letter we found in the study of Cooper."

Rubens face went pale. He looked in horror from one to the other. "So, it was you?" he stammered. "You were the ones who –"

"The letter," continued Mr G, "is sent by Hopkins and on it is written the name Keach." He let out an exasperated sigh. "Now, we both know that Hopkins and Cooper were hiding some of the bounty. But the one I am interested now, is Keach." He moved his face close to Rubens. "If you had connection with Hopkins you would certainly have known this man." He gripped the fat man by the throat. "Now, I will ask you again, Mister Rubens. Where can I find Keach?"

The silversmith's face turned from a glowing pink to an unhealthy shade of purple. His eyes began to protrude from their sockets as Groot tightened his grip.

Almost a minute passed before he let go. Rubens threw his head back in an attempt to catch his breath; the sound of his gasps giving much amusement to his visitors. Without remorse they mimicked the poor man's desperate efforts to fill his lungs.

Mr G cocked his head to one side and held up his hand. "Hush!" he whispered.

All went quiet. Rubens' gasps settled to a gentle wheezing sound.

Outside the room, somewhere in the hall below, there was another sound. Of course they knew Jack was down there. If there was one thing the skinny man was accomplished at, it was stealth. But there was definitely someone else down below.

Footsteps on the stairs now. The Frenchman slipped behind the door.

Mr G took his pistol from his belt and pulled back the hammer. He pressed the barrel against the side of Ruben's head. "One sound and your skull will be splinters!"

The bed-chamber was silent.

All three men held their breath as the footsteps reached the landing.

"Mister Rubin?" a female voice called.

"Mister Rubin, you is all right?" she repeated. Her words tinted with an accent – not English.

The gun was pressed against the fat man's head.

"Mister Rubin, I think you is not all right," the voice persisted.

The latch clicked and the door swung open. Standing outside, holding up a lamp, was a young dark-skinned woman dressed in the attire of a housemaid. Her hand shot up to her mouth.

Jack stepped up from behind. "In you go, my pretty!" He took the lamp from the girl's hand and shoved her into Mr Ruben's bed-chamber.

Pierre appeared from behind the door, his face beaming with delight.

Chapter 9 – **Morning Dues**

The morning sun had been up for more than two hours when Toby first stirred from the *lit a repose*. He tried to adjust his eyes. The parting in the drapes at the window was barely four fingers wide but enough to allow the sunlight to flood into the room. He attempted to sit up but his head pounded like an anvil. He looked down. His clothes were in disarray; shirt open to his belt, breeches undone at the front. He hastily adjusted himself as he tried to recall the events of the previous evening.

The dance. Did he dream it? Their movements had been so graceful, as if they were floating in air. Could he have imagined it all? He must have been taken by fantasy, for the two women appeared to undress each other in his presence; a skirt removed, a petticoat falling to the floor, a corset untied – how could this be real?

Toby looked around. The room was quiet. There appeared to be no-one there. With great determination, he lifted himself up from the sofa. The table was littered with plates of half-eaten food. The bed had been disturbed, yet there were no clothes or personal items around. His guests must have gone. He checked his pockets. Where was his purse? He lifted cushions, moved chairs, even searched the adjoining room! Toby steadied himself to look under the bed. His head exploded like a canon. He slumped into a chair at the table. It was obvious now. He'd been robbed!

Resting his elbows on the table, Toby sunk his head into his hands. How could he have been so stupid! He squeezed his eyes in an attempt to clear his throbbing head. When he opened them he focussed on the items on the table; an untidy assortment of wine glasses, pewter plates, bowls, a quill and a sheet of paper. The paper was weighted down by a small goatskin bag – his purse! Toby quickly picked it up and emptied the contents. Several gold escudos and silver coins rolled out. After the third attempt Toby was satisfied that the total, after deducting the previous day's expenses, was approximately what he expected. He picked up the paper and screwed his eyes at the neatly scribed words.

My dear sweet Toby. Both Beatrice and myself thank you for your most gracious hospitality and we hope that you find yourself in good health and spirits once you have rested. You will find your money bag here with this letter. Not wishing to disturb you this morning, I have taken the liberty of deducting two escudos being the amount due for the employment of our company. I hope this is in order. Beatrice has asked me to give you directions to the house of her Aunt which I have copied below. Should you require our services in the future, you may contact us through the proprietor, Madame Leticia. We both hope that you will do so. Your loyal and loving friend, Elizabeth Thomas.

Toby threw the letter back to the table. Whores! Why had he not seen it? How could he have been so fooled by their masquerade of deceit?

Chapter 10 – La Bruma

The sun was already over the hill behind the farm in Saint Andrews. Magdalena was standing at the window in the hall. She got her first sight of Master Toby as he came around the bend at the far side of the hollow. She knew it was him by the way he made his way along the track. "Lord God, look at you boy!" the woman muttered. "Lookin' this way, lookin' that, you is just like your father." Handsome too, she thought. And big. He a man now, got to be more than twenty-five year. Funny how Mister Edward say his daughter be the one to come. And now it too late for he to know. Magdalena shook her head. Such a thing The Lord take Mister Edward before he see his boy all grown up.

The young man walked on past the gates, studied the note in his hand, hesitated, then turned back. He stood at the end of the carriageway for a good while, shielding his eyes from the sun as he stared up towards the house.

Magdalena stepped back from the window. What is you thinkin', boy? It too untidy? Too much a mess to be your father's house? Mister Edward use to say his house in London like a palace. All loved and cared for like you would care for a baby, he'd say. Magdalena sucked through her teeth. That all well and good when you got servants to make it nice. She gave a quick glance around the hall; linen sheets covered the few remaining items, grey and mysterious behind the closed shutters. A layer of fine sand, brought in by the storms, covered the floor. How can she keep this all nice by herself when she have a child to care for? She ain't getin' no help here; all the land boys run away to the hills after

Mister Edward gone. And they don't come back too, not one of them.

Magdalena pressed her face to the slats of the shuttered door. Mother of God, he coming now! She stepped back and hastily tidied her skirts.

The noise above her head made her heart jump. Magdalena looked up at the bell above the door. Long time since that been shakin'. She was waiting for the spring to settle when a young boy came running into the hall, his bare feet slapping against the stone floor.

"Mama, c'est hombre a la puerta! (A man at the door!)"

Magdalena quickly swept up the boy into her arms.

"Hush child!" she whispered. "Parla nada! Stay quiet Edo!"

The figure on the porch loomed close to the door. Magdalena moved quickly to the side and pressed a finger to her lips. Both she and her son listened to the grating of iron as the bell chain settled inside its casing.

Toby pulled the bell-chain again and waited . . . no reply. The sign at the gate definitely indicated that this house was La Bruma. He frowned at the broken strut on the shutter, down at the dark green shoots pushing their way through the decking. The place looked as if it had been abandoned, yet he was sure he heard a child's voice calling. Toby peered through the slatted door; too dark to see inside but it could be possible there was someone there. He stepped down from the porch and was half way down the path when the grating of a metal bolt made him turn back. The door opened a fraction, then jammed. Fat fingers wrapped around the frame and yanked. Toby moved forward to help.

"No, leave it! It come," came a voice from inside. A final tug and the heavy wooden door gave way onto a dark hall.

The woman, a Negro with a child at her side, filled the doorway with her large frame. Toby was about to explain the reason for his visit when, without a word, the woman vanished into the darkness. She must be the housekeeper, he thought; gone to find her master. But then she didn't even venture to ask his name: not been properly trained.

A moment later the woman reappeared. "You not comin'?" she frowned.

Toby stepped into a large entrance hall, difficult to see on account of the shutters being closed. He followed the echo of the woman's sandals as they shuffled across sand-dusted tiles towards an open doorway to the right. The child following close to his mother, kept a suspicious eye on Toby as he was led down a long narrow passage to the kitchen at the rear of the house.

While of good size, the room was sparsely furnished; a workbench, a plain table and two chairs. There was a door and a window which looked out onto a barren field rising from the rear of the house.

The woman set down her child in the corner where various wooden toys littered the floor. She turned and pointed Toby to a chair.

"You like molasses water?"

"Yes I do." Toby sat down. "If it not be too much trouble for you."

The child's mother chuckled as she took a cup and poured out water from a large jug.

"You talk like your father," she laughed.

Toby watched her stir in the molasses with slow deliberate movements. He frowned. "How do you know who I am? I did not –"

"Bea say you is comin'. She not tell you how to find me?"

"Beatrice? Well, yes she did."

"Then, that how I know." The woman placed the cup in front of Toby and returned to busy herself at the workbench. Like so many Negroes of her age, she had let herself go; wide hips and well padded rear, thick shapeless ankles protruding beneath her shrunken skirts. And that dress! The woman must have had it for years; seams split at the back, and the pattern, once set with bright colours was now washed out to an ochre grey. Does she not wish to purchase new clothes?

He took a sip of the sweetened water. "You spoke of my father. I have been trying to discover where he is. I only learnt a week ago that he lives here in Jamaica."

"He live?" She turned to look at him. "You not know?"

"Not know what?"

The woman didn't reply for a while. From a bucket on the floor she took what looked to be a cassava. Her arms, which at first seemed as firm as leather, shook with every movement as she scraped away at the husk . "The Lord take your father away."

"What Lord?"

Again, the woman didn't respond but continued her scraping until the white of the root was completely exposed. Using the weight of her upper body, she rubbed the tuber vigorously against a metal grater reducing the core to a pulp. The whole process was then repeated. It was more than a minute before she spoke again.

"Your father, he dead."

Toby stared at the cup turning in his hands. "Was he afflicted with an illness?"

"No. It not that."

The woman came to sit at the table. "He killed by maroons in the hills."

"Maroons?"

"Them that fights for freedom." She looked down at the floor. "But they not all bad. Only some."

She told Toby how Captain Hopkins was called up to protect the folk in a village. How some maroons had been killing innocent slaves who refused to join them. A rebel who had been waiting in ambush, fired a single shot. Toby's father died instantly.

"When was this?"

"Six year past."

Toby tried to estimate the age of the boy playing in the corner of the room.

"How did you know my father?"

The woman made a sucking noise through her teeth. "I live with him two year before he taken from me." She looked towards the boy playing quietly with his toys. "This his son."

His skin was a tone lighter than his mother. His hair, dark and a little wavy, was not unlike his father's. But he had his mother's eyes; dark brown, thoughtful.

"What's his name?"

"Eduardo."

So, his father's name lives on. Toby was touched. "Did my father choose that name?"

The woman had her back to him. She took a deep breath. "His father not know him. He born after Mister Edward die."

Toby shuffled uncomfortably in his chair. He could tell this was difficult for the woman, but what should he do? Toby remained seated and hoped that she would soon regain her composure. "Did my father tell you about my family... his family, in England?"

"Yes, he think. . ." She cleared her throat. "He think you all dead in a fire. He love you. Love you like you all was his angels." She put her work to one side and sat at the table. "He always tell me 'bout you." She nodded to the boy in the corner. "Eduardo your brother now." She made a move to take Toby's hand, but then withdrew.

Toby stood up and moved to the kitchen window. Outside, a field of flattened cane covered the hill, dried to a cinder by the baking sun. He considered what this woman had been saying: that she and her son were now his closest living relatives. This was not what he expected. He needed time to take it aboard. Could this woman be trusted? He turned from the window and studied her. "I don't know your name?"

"Magdalena."

"Is this your land?" he asked.

"Your father's. . . Yours now." The woman got up and resumed her work at the bench. "What your little sister name?" she asked.

"Sister?" Toby was puzzled. He glanced at the boy playing in the corner. "Do you mean, Eduardo?"

"No, no," Magdalena laughed. "Your sister in England, what her name?"

"Oh, you mean Ann... and Mary. Two sisters "

"That it, Mary." The woman turned back to her work. "I remember now, Ann and Mary," she repeated. "It break Mister Edward heart when he hear about the fire."

Toby shuffled his feet. The last thing he wanted to do was recount the subject of the fire. Related or not, the woman was hardly someone with whom he was sufficiently acquainted to discuss such personal matters.

"Did my father not remember anything about us, other than that?" Toby made no attempt to hide his sardonic tone.

"Oh Lord yes! He tell me all 'bout how you all learn good and 'bout all the games you play together."

"Games?"

"Yes, games you play when you was little." Magdalena cocked her head to one side. There was a long pause as she fixed her look on him. "You not remember?"

Toby tried to think back.

The woman shook her head and took another cassava root from the bucket. "How long you stay here?" she asked.

"The last ferry boat to Port Royal returns just before nightfall. I need not return until then. But if I am being an intrusion –"

"No, it fine you stay," she chuckled. "I not ask that. I say, how long in Jamaica?"

"Oh, I see. I intend to leave before the next week. . . if I should find a suitable vessel."

"You is a sailor?"

Toby told his story; a similar account to the one he told to Elizabeth at *The King's Rose* the evening before. He mentioned the fire. However, as soon as he said it, he wished he hadn't, for bringing up these details evoked some painful emotions upon himself. He searched for a change in topic. "How old is your niece?" he asked.

"Bea?"

"Yes."

"She twenty years come December." Magdalena smiled. "She a good girl, very clever."

Toby considered this appraisal of the girl with whom he had spent the previous night. Is she clever? Maybe she is. But is she good? Toby concluded that Beatrice may not be telling all to her aunt.

Eduardo, now tired of his game stood beside his mother and tugged at her skirts. She handed him a cup of molasses and nodded towards their guest. "Esta Toby, seu frère. (This is Toby, your brother)."

"He can speak French?" Toby asked.

"Frañol, I teach him some English too."

"Frañol?"

"Francaise-Español. French some, Spanish some." She turned to the boy. "Say hello to Mister Toby, mi petit."

Eduardo, who had not said a word to Toby since his arrival, responded with an air of confidence. "Ola."

"Hello, young soldier," Toby shook the boy by the hand. Eduardo beamed and went back to playing quietly in the corner. His mother picked another cassava from the bucket.

What did his father see in this woman? She is no different to any other of her kind: lazy to the bone! What has she done about the upkeep of the estate over the years? Nothing! Just left the place to ruin. Here was an opportunity to improve herself, to rise above her station. But no, as soon as her master is gone, she does nothing but shuffle from room to room. And what will become of her son? His father's son, Toby's half brother. What kind of future will *he* have?

The boy was tired, even Toby could tell. Refusing to sleep, Eduardo lay on the floor, head resting on the stone tiles, eyes fixed on the little wooden boat he pushed along the floor: a two-masted barque setting out to far distant shores. The model was perfect in every way: rigging, masts, stays, all crafted in detail: certainly not a child's toy.

Toby crouched down next to him.

Eduardo, dark eyes seeking approval, placed the model gently into his hand. His skin tone was almost the same tone as Toby's tanned fingers.

"Mister Edward make it." Magdalena, who had been watching them, spoke with pride.

Toby studied the vessel. He had often watched John Fowler, the *Chesapeake's* Mate, make these models and could appreciate how much time and effort his father must have spent on this one. "Esta barca bonita – a beautiful ship," he said to the boy.

Eduardo's eyes lit up as Toby handed the model back.

Magdalena shuffled towards the door. "You stay here," she said. "I show you something."

Toby watched his half-brother push the boat along the bare tiles. When Magdalena returned she was carrying a box which she put aside. From this, she took out a little wooden flute and placed it on the table. One glance was enough for Toby. He felt a lump rise in his throat and had to squeeze his eyes to hold back the tears.

"You know what it is?" Magdalena rested her hand gently on his shoulder.

"Yes." Toby took a breath. "I made it for my father when I was seven."

"When you was seven?" The woman raised her eyebrows.

"No, I was ten, I believe."

But I thought Mister Edward say you big sister make it."

"Yes, we each made him one." Toby looked closely at the detail. "This is mine, I am sure of it."

"Why you make him this?"

"It was just before he left to go to Virginia." Toby felt the tears rise up again. "I wanted to give him something to remember me."

Magdalena gave his shoulder a squeeze. "This for you," she handed him the box and moved back to the bench. "Your papa ask me to keep for you 'cos he not believe all of you is taken in the fire."

Toby's fingers followed the shape of the box as if it might fall apart in his hands.

Magdalena lifted Eduardo up and took his hand. At the door she turned to Toby. "Me and Edo go an' cut guava. You stay here." She pointed towards the top of the field. "You find us out back when you is ready."

Toby took out the contents of the box and, one by one, laid each item out on the table; a ring, a collection of letters tied in a ribbon and a little sketch of the house in Lombard Street. At the bottom was a sheet of paper. Toby unfolded it and recognised his father's writing:

To my dearest Isabella and my three beautiful children. I am writing this letter to you in the hope that you are alive and well and that one day we will be re-united. Despite having sent many letters to our house in Lombard Street, I have not received a reply from you for over a year now and, perish the thought, since news has reached here of a great fire in the city, I fear the worst fate has become thee. I pray to God each day that my fears are unfounded. My duties here in the colonies are arduous and fraught with many dangers and should Our Lord decide that my time on this earth be no longer, I shall leave this letter in the trusted hands of my loyal servant Magdalena, a close and loving friend to me for the past two years, with the confidence that she will pass it to you. Of my dear sweet children my thoughts are with you every day. I always remember the rhyme of the miller's wife we sometimes used to sing and I think so fondly of that little game we played together when seeking the painted eggs on Easter day. Do you remember? I have written a new set at the end of this letter so that we can play it together even if I am no longer there to join you. Of you Isabella I have a vision as a loving and caring mother to my three darling children, Ann, Toby and little Mary. A picture which I will always keep in my heart. Your ever loving husband and father, Edward James Hopkins.

Here follows the game

aI3eIII3a4,eIII3bII3b2cI4f1eV1fI5bI6fI3,eV1,dI6vcI1bII3b2eI6 aI2eIII3b1bII3a2eIV3aII3fV3eVI3,fIII1.b1fV3c3fI1,cI4dII4bI6fII I2d2aII4eIII3,1668,d3eIV4fVI1bII1eIV2d2aI4fVII1bII4fI2f2.xaI2 fI6.b3fI6a2fI6e3f1,fI4e2cI6,d12fII1,eIII3fII1eII1aII1gvd1.eV1bII 2fI3,bI5,eII1

While these heartfelt words may have offered an explanation to many of the questions Toby had been pondering over the years, he felt little emotion upon reading them. However, at the mention of his mother and siblings, he broke. Tears flowed down his face, sobs that were so forceful and violent that he thought his heart would seize. It took many minutes before Toby could breathe again. He got up from the table and stepped through the door where Magdelena ans Eduardo had left.

Once he stepped outside he felt more at ease and less of an intruder. For the next hour Toby felt at liberty to roam around the farm and get his bearings of the home of his late father.

The property covered an area of about three acres – small in comparison to the plantations Toby had passed on his way that morning but not without its unique charm. The land, however, had suffered serious neglect over the years; the worst being the large field which ran up the hill to the rear of the main house. The clods of dry earth, when trodden under foot, crushed to a fine red dust and the whole field was covered with brittle cane. In contrast, the areas which bordered this barren field were abundant. So fertile was the copse that ran up to the left side of the field that Toby found it impossible to pass through the tangle of vines and creepers that clung to the shrubs and trees here. He tried to identify some of the plants here and, while he recognised the banana and birch, there were some trees further inside this wood that were new to him. He was curious to know how this area could be so prolific and yet the field lay so barren and dry.

Once he reached the top of the hill, Toby had a good view of the house and two stone-built outbuildings that led away to the right. Now the sun was in full force, these looked cool and inviting, so he made his way back down. Before inspecting the outbuildings, he took the path which ran alongside the main house and led to the front. Here, the row of trees which bordered the front approach looked particularly elegant: one of the first things he noticed when he arrived that morning. However, the ground cover was overgrown and needed much work.

The house was in need of some urgent repair; a number of dislodged roof tiles and places where the cladding had come away from the front wall. Some fresh paintwork to the existing window shutters and renovation of the porch would also improve the appearance of the place. If these alterations were to be made they would certainly enhance the approach to the property. The repairs would take a few months to complete and would also demand funds which he didn't have. What should he do? He had to ensure that his crew, or what was left of them, secure a safe passage to their homes in Virginia and Maryland. The fluyt moored out in the bay, although a bargain, was still more than he could afford. He would need to raise funds to purchase it or a similar vessel somehow if he was to get back it his homeland. John may be interested in making a joint venture. He will have to wait and see. But he now had a family here in Jamaica. Toby could remain here instead. Should he stay or go?

He stood on the front path and looked out across the valley and beyond to the distant town of Port Royal with its sheltered and well defended harbour: a prosperous centre for any ambitious trader. It then occurred to him – why not do both – make this his new home, a base for his trading ventures with the northern colonies.

With this new resolve Toby made his way back to the rear of the building.

Chapter 11 – **Childhood Games**

The kitchen was empty when he returned. Again he picked up the note from his father, this time avoiding the words which had disturbed him so much and studied the code at the end of the letter. Baffled by his father's reference to a game, he tried to recall all the songs of his childhood. He looked for a paper and quill: nothing in this room.

Left alone in the house, he ventured down the passageway that led to the hall. Now his eyes were accustomed to the dark, he was able to discern several items of furniture covered with linen sheets like wild beasts waiting for the closed season to end. With care, he lifted the corner of the nearest which sent up a cloud of dust to gradually settle on the floor. It felt a little strange to be standing alone in this place; as if he were an intruder not wishing to be discovered. And yet, hadn't Magdalena said all this was rightly his now? Funny to think of her as his step-mother. But could this really be so? Probably not. She hadn't actually married his father so she was no more than a house-keeper. What if the woman had made the whole story up? He only had her word for it. There was no record of his father's death in the cemetery in Port Royal. He pulled the cover further back to reveal a finely crafted oak table; probably imported from Boston and certainly of a better quality than anything he had seen in Port Royal. But, there again, he only arrived in Jamaica two days ago and neither he, nor his crew had visited here before: hardly time to make such bold judgement. He replaced the sheet and brushed the dust from the floor with the sole of his shoe. The tile under his foot was an intricate design in yellow and blue; a Portuguese motif which was repeated on every other tile throughout the hall. He looked around the room. He hadn't noticed the stairs when he was first shown into the house and, now his eyes had adjusted to the dark, he could see the steps and balustrade of a splendid staircase sculptured from rosewood. Ascending to a half-mezzanine landing, the structure then divided into two stairways which curved to the upper floor. Most of the furniture on the ground floor was in excellent condition and appeared to have been imported either from England or the Northern colonies. Toby could only presume his father would have been privileged to be able to afford all this. Would he have really wished to leave it all in the care of his Negro housekeeper? Not that he had much choice: his death was untimely. Despite these thoughts, Toby still had the feeling he was encroaching on Magdalena's territory and thought it better to look for the woman and her son. Her son? Eduardo, his half brother? Could this really be true? After searching for so long for his estranged father, to learn that he had died six years before, was more than enough for Toby. But, after grieving the loss of his mother and two sisters for the past nine years, to be told, in the same day, that he now has a step mother and a half brother was difficult to take aboard.

Toby returned along the path to the back of the house where he was met by Magdalena armed with a heavy machete and Eduardo wheeling a cart half-filled with green and red fruit not unlike English apples.

"Come, we make guava ready for market," Magdalena said.

Eduardo brought the cart to a halt alongside a trestle-table which stood under the shade of a tree next to the door of the kitchen. With Magdalena's guidance, all three sorted the fruit into groups, placing the best in wooden trays ready to take to the market in St Jago.

Toby watched Eduardo as they worked together in silence. The boy was quick; making short work of sorting the fruit. How sad to hear that his father had died before knowing his son. He considered his visit to the militia office the previous day; how uncooperative the sergeant had been. Surely it would have been a simple matter to tell Toby that his father had been shot while on commission; it would have saved him the time and embarrassment of the previous evening.

He glanced at Magdalena; the dark skin of her fleshy arms rippling as she tapped each fruit before placing it in the tray. He thought of his meeting with the two women, Elizabeth and Beatrice, at the King's Rose the evening before. Had he not given word of the search for his father, then he would not be here now.

Some of the ripened guava Magdalena put aside and it was later that evening, after a generous helping of yuca bread and baked fish, that Toby was to have his first taste of this refreshing fruit.

After supper Toby was left alone at the kitchen table while Magdalena took Eduardo to his room. He had time to reflect on the past few days. A doubt began to enter his thoughts; the fanciful words of Jack Bride, the notion that Toby's father was living in Jamaica, the evasive answers of the sergeant at the militia office, and the meeting with Elizabeth and Beatrice.

Was it not strange that all these events had taken place as soon as Toby arrived in Port Royal. What if all this was a wicked plot? Was it not more than coincidence that, the moment Toby announced he was on a quest to find his father, two whores in the house of Madame Leticia made his acquaintance. Not only that, but how convenient that one of them happened to have an aunt, a Negro woman, who, not only knew his father, but had given birth to his child. An evil plot indeed. Particularly when Toby, in earnest, had disclosed the full story of his past life in England and reference to the tragic loss of his mother and two sisters when the fire swept through Lombard Street.

But to what purpose? After all, Toby had made it plain that he had no money; had given account of the sinking of his vessel in Maracaibo and the loss of his trading business. So, what reason could there be to engage him into a ruse? Surely he had nothing to offer them.

But why was Magdalena keen for him to stay? He could easily have caught the return ferry to Port Royal that evening and taken a room at the inn where the remainder of his crew were lodging. But the woman had insisted that he stay at the farm. Was this a token of her hospitality? Toby doubted it. He tried to recall the conversation with the woman that afternoon. There was something. She had been confused about his sisters' names, but Toby sensed that this was just a test to see if he was an imposter. That idea alone made Toby more suspicious: why would his identity be of such importance. But there was something else; something the woman was curious to know. His thoughts were interrupted when Magdalena returned. She said little, apart from suggesting she show him the upper floor of the house.

There were four good sized rooms up there, one of which was a guest room furnished with a solid and comfortable bed, and further down the landing, an office. This room was small, compact with a window overlooking the road and valley to the front of the house. Along the wall, close to the window, was a bookcase holding several volumes bound in vermilion and royal blue. Across from the bookcase was a maple bureau desk and a chair. Magdalena pulled open a drawer of the bureau, took out a sheet of cream paper, and laid it on the desk. She lifted the inkwell from its holder and filled it from a brown jug tucked away in the corner of the room. Toby was intrigued by the way this woman went about these preparations; slow and deliberate, as if she been familiar with the routine for years. She took a long rectangular case from the drawer and carefully opened the lid. Inside, resting on a bed of velvet was a goose quill pen.

Before she left the room, Toby ventured to ask where his father was laid to rest.

"La Cruz Roja."

He was puzzled.

"The old church in Santiago. We go every Sunday. . . me an' Edo."

Once she had gone Toby sat at the desk. He imagined his father doing the same. From here he could look out onto the road which he had walked along that morning. And in the distance, beyond the edge of the hill, he had a fine view of the bay and the harbour of Port Royal.

He took his father's letter from the box and read it though again. *To my dearest Isabella and my three beautiful children . . . I always remember the rhyme of the miller's wife we sometimes used to sing and I think so fondly of that little game we played together when seeking the painted eggs on Easter day. Do you remember? I have written a new set at the end of this letter so that we can play it together even if I am no longer there to join you . . .*

That was it! Magdalena had asked him about the games he used to play as a child; the game his father referred to in the letter. But surely the woman couldn't read: how would she know about that? There must be something important about this reference for his father to be so pressing about it. He copied down the code.

For a good while Toby studied the opening symbols: *al3elII3a4.* Tried as he did to remember a rhyme about a miller's wife, he just couldn't recall one. Without this information, the code would be of no use to anyone. He folded the letter and returned it to the box. Before leaving, he looked through the volumes in the bookcase and took down one with the title *Lucasta; a collection of poems by Richard Lovelace.* With this tucked under his arm, he went out to the landing and the guest room Magdalena had shown him earlier. Within ten minutes the book had fallen from his fingers to the floor beside his bed and Toby was asleep.

For as long as he could remember Toby had not slept so well as he had that night; no waking at every sound with concern for the security of his valuables or his own safety, no interruptions with suggestion of violence in the street below (the only disturbance being the early morning call from the parrots in the valley). But most of all, Toby was not visited by the horrors of the dream which had not spared him a night for months. For once he awoke refreshed. He rose from his bed with an enthusiastic outlook for the day ahead.

Magdalena was at her usual station at the workbench in the kitchen.

"Good day, Magdalena."

The woman turned to him with a look of surprise. "Well, Mister Toby. Your legs is not broke?" she chuckled. "I think you is never gonna wake."

"Oh, please forgive me." Toby looked out to the window and the sunlit field beyond. He took the chair at the table. "I did not realise the hour was so late."

"Aye, aye, aye," Magdalena laughed and shook her head. "You is always sayin' you is sorry." She wiped her hands on the front of her dress and stepped over to Toby. She reached out and squeezed his hand. "There ain't no need for that."

Embarrassed, Toby wished to move away but the warmth of her touch held him like a spell.

"You ain't do nothin' wrong." She released him and moved back to the bench. "Edo, he look for you." She nodded towards the window. "He up top of field."

Toby made a move to get up.

"No, no. You eat first." Magdalena broke off a piece of cassava bread. She drew up a chair and handed it to him.

Somewhat uncomfortable Toby was aware of this woman sitting across the table watching him eat.

"Why you come to Jamaica?"

Relieved to take his mind away from the omnipresent scrutiny of his eating habits, Toby was happy to relate his story of events which led him too Jamaica.

Magdalena sat and listened without saying a word.

Toby expected her to comment but she remained silent as if deep in thought. He finished the bread and got up from the table. Before he left Magdalena asked how long he intended to stay at the farm.

"I'm not sure. I don't wish to be an intrusion."

"Intrusion?" Magdalena giggled. "Boy, you talk real funny."

Toby was about to explain when it occurred to him that it was possible the woman understood far more than she let on.

The wooded area which bordered the left of the field opened out along the top of the hill to form a dense impenetrable tangle of scrub land. Eduardo was crouched down behind a fig tree at the edge of the scrub. The boy pressed a finger to his lips and beckoned to Toby.

About a dozen yards beyond the banana plants and ferns was a clearing with a few widely spaced trees. Something was moving amongst the long grass. At first it looked like a stray dog, but when it made an appearance into the open it showed itself to be a wild pig. The little animal was busy scraping away between the roots of a large tree, pausing on occasion to survey the surroundings before burying its muzzle into the soft earth.

Edo, eyes shining with excitement, turned to Toby and made a sign with his hand to his mouth. "Bueno para comer," he said.

It hadn't occurred to Toby that the boy's objective was to procure a meal from the poor little hog. He considered that he may be able persuade him to catch the animal and keep it alive, in a pen perhaps. He was about to suggest this when Edo shot out from his hiding place, scrambled through the bushes and ran into the clearing. The pig, on hearing the commotion, removed its snout from the burrow and without a second glance, headed for the scrub as fast as its little legs would take it.

Edo, downcast, kicked at the ground as he made his way back across the clearing. Toby tried his best to console him, but to no avail. Then he had an idea.

During the time of his indenture in Maryland, Toby had planted a crop of maize which happened to be adjacent to a plot worked by a man named Will. Due to the troubles with the Indians, Will had given up his fur-trapping business and tried to make a living by farming the soil. It so happened at that time, Toby's own land was continually invaded by some illusive creature which was determined to destroy his crop. Will, having a sense for animal behaviour, was the first to discover the cause of the problem: raccoons. The trapper also came up with a solution and showed Toby how to go about catching the culprits.

Toby made a digging motion to Eduardo.

The boy, still affected by his recent failure, shrugged his shoulders and signalled for Toby to follow him down the hill. Minutes later they were back at the clearing with two shovels and the little hand cart.

Starting a couple of paces away from the roots of the tree, Toby began to dig a hole about four feet by two while Eduardo took the smaller spade and filled the cart from the mound of soft earth. Within an hour a hole to the depth of three feet was complete. From the copse they both collected some thin branches and placed them across the top of the trench followed by a layer of banana leaves.

"What we need now is something to entice our quarry to the lair."

"Que?" The boy gave Toby a quizzical look.

Toby pointed to the centre of the covering and did his best to repeat the phrase in Spanish.

Edo gave a satisfied smile. "Vamos, Mister Toby!"

They were about half way down the track when the boy asked Toby what the word for *vamos* was in English.

"Let's go!" said Toby.

"Les-go!" repeated Edo.

They both laughed.

And so it was then, Toby decided he would stay at the farm until Friday.

Chapter 12 – **Ruben's Bedchamber**

The air in Aaron Rubens' bedchamber in Port Royal was thick and putrid. It was Friday, the fourth day of October. Sergeant Smithson had been looking forward to enjoying time with his family for the next three days. Due to recent developments connected with the case, all immediate leave for Smithson and his assistant, Corporal Jones, had been cancelled.

A mid-morning sun streamed through the window which looked out over the tiled rooftops of New Street. Several flies, disturbed by the visitors, buzzed impatiently around the room.

"Right, Jones, you can cover her up now." Sergeant Smithson straightened up.

His assistant took one short step towards the foot of the bed. "Er, where shall I put these notes, Sir?"

Smithson glanced up at his pale face. "Don't worry, Jones, I'll do it," he sighed.

Stripped to the waist, the girl had been bound by the ankles and wrists to the four corners of her master's bed while Mr Rubens, had been secured to the chair which was placed in the centre of the room. Papers and documents were scattered over the floor.

Smithson fastened the front of the girl's chemise over her blood-stained breasts. "We've seen enough here."

Jones headed for the door.

"Before we leave, Corporal, it'll be a good idea to run through everything."

"Don't we usually do that back at the fort, Sarge?"

The investigations had been attracting attention from all ranks at Fort Charles and Smithson wondered if he and Jones were becoming the subject of ridicule.

"Well, yes, you're right, Jones. However, it'll be more peaceful here. You know, no interruptions and the like."

"Can we go down to the lower floor then, Sir?" The corporal was holding his nose and fanning himself with his board.

"Good point, Jones." Smithson took one last look around the room and followed his assistant out onto the landing.

At the floor below the Sergeant stopped outside a closed door. "Have you had a look in here?"

"Aye, Sir. The maid's quarters. Nothing to suggest who she is though."

"Hum."

They continued down to the ground floor.

The back door was unlocked when Smithson and his assistant first arrived. In the kitchen there was another which was connected to the silversmith's shop. This door was locked and there was no sign of forced entry.

The two investigators settled down at the kitchen table.

"What do you make of this one, Jones?"

The corporal studied his notes.

"I'd say they've been dead a couple of days."

"How come?"

"Because Mister Rubens didn't turn up at the customs house on Thursday morning like he always does and he was last seen in Madame Leticia's Residence, The King's Rose, on Wednesday evening."

The Sergeant nodded. "So, that would likely make this killing sometime on the Wednesday night, then." Smithson paused. "I'd say it quite likely he let the perpetrators in himself. Can you go back to Leticia's tonight and see if anyone was with him?"

"Yes, Sir."

The sergeant stroked his side whiskers. Why would someone want all these people killed? he thought. He turned to his assistant. "Can you see a connection betwixt the victims, Jones?"

The corporal rested his board at the edge of the table. "Well, Sir. They were all officers in the militia."

"All except for this one," said Smithson.

"Exactly, Sir."

"Do you have any doubts that Mister Rubens and the poor girl were killed by the same person as committed the other murders?"

"I'd say they were, Sir."

"In that case, there must be some chain which links the victims together."

"Robbery of sorts?"

"There hasn't been valuables reported missing. Did you notice any items in his room up there?"

"Yes, Sir. A candle holder resting in the window. Looked like it was silver."

"So, if the perpetrator has no intention of taking valuables, what is he after?"

"He, Sir?"

"Good point, Jones. What if it's a woman, seeking revenge maybe?"

"I don't think a woman would be capable of –"

"No, quite. But, how about if these acts are committed by more than one person?"

"Most likely, I'd say, Sarge."

"If you remember, the young lad at Colonel Brown's house said he heard more than one person there."

Smithson set a flame to his pipe, a bubbling sound emitting from the stem as he sucked. "They're certainly looking for something, Jones. Information, maybe?"

"That would explain the mess of papers up in his room. Just like at the other killings too."

Smithson frowned. He pulled out a paper from his pocket and laid it on the table.

"What's that, Sir?"

"Best you don't know, least not for now, Jones." The sergeant studied the list of names he had taken from the home of Colonel Brown, the previous victim in Spanish Town. Of the men enlisted on *The Trident,* six were officers of the militia. In addition to Lieutenant Cooper and Captain Rogers, the colonel's name was there, plus three others; Lieutenant John Burns, Major James Stead and Captain Edward Hopkins.

Smithson searched the remaining names but there was no reference to an Aaron Rubens. He folded the paper and put it back in his pocket. "I want you to find out if this man Rubens has any connection with privateering activities. Particularly with the raids on Portobello in sixty-eight."

"Yes, Sir." Corporal Jones scribbled a few notes with his new pencil stick.

"There is also a letter, you will find it amongst the items collected at the Cooper investigation. It's a note written to Cooper by a Captain Hopkins which –"

"I have it here, Sir."

Smithson raised an eyebrow. "You have the letter?"

"Yes, Sir. It's here somewhere" Jones searched though the papers attached to his board. "Ah, this is it."

The sergeant blew a thin stream of smoke in the air. He took the letter and placed it flat on the table.

La Bruma, Saint Andrews, Twentyeth August 1669

My dear William, I hope this finds you and Charlotte in good health and that your duties in Barbadoes are not too arduous. Life here is as much of a routine as always with the occasional skirmish with the maroons and usual incidents in the town to see to, but nothing to match our diversions in Portobello. However, some exciting news, As you see from the address I have acquired a property, a farm in the parish of Saint Andrew with views looking out to PR harbour. The air up here is so clean and fresh and I have to confess living in the countryside so much an improvement to life in Port Royal. I have also taken on a house keeper, a free negro who has lived in Jamaica since the Spanish were here. She is a kindly woman and is also proving to be a great asset to the running of the farm. With regards to our prize, we can hold our mutual interest with Rogers. He has good connections in Port Royal and will know what to do. As for the remainder, I would suggest we leave this in the capable hands of Keach until you return. I look forward to seeing you both. Tell Charlotte the garden at Villa Madre is looking very colourful and she can be assured I am attending to it each week. Your loyal and loving friend, Edward Hopkins.

"This letter was written over two years before Cooper and his wife were murdered. It was found open on his desk during the investigation." Smithson took a couple of sucks on his pipe. "So, it would appear the perpetrators of the crime also had an interest in the content, wouldn't you say so?"

"I would, Sir, yes."

The sergeant pushed the letter across the table to his assistant and waited for him to read it through. "What do you think, Jones?"

"To the advantages of living in the countryside, Sir?"

"Very funny, Jones. What do you make of the reference to name Keach?"

"I have considered this, Sarge. I can only think it was a mutual friend of Mister Hopkins and Lieutenant Cooper."

Smithson reached inside his jerkin and pulled out the paper he had been reading earlier. He ran down the list of names, sighed, shook his head and returned it to his pocket.

"You asked me for my thoughts on the connections between the victims, Sir," Jones said.

"Yes, go on."

"Well, if the person, or persons, who killed Cooper had been reading his correspondence then they would have seen the reference to Captain Rogers."

"Your point is?"

"Rogers was murdered in July this year, Sir."

"Yes, I know, we were both assigned to the case, remember?" Smithson raised his eyes to the heavens. "Get to the point, Jones."

"Forgive me, Sir, but why did it take them nearly four years to get to Captain Rogers?"

Smithson removed his pipe from his lips and stabbed the air. "I wish I knew the answer to that one, Jones. I wish I knew."

Chapter 13 – New Recruits

On the Friday at noon as arranged, John Fowler, the Mate of the fateful *Chesapeake Venture*, was found sitting on a bench outside the Spar and Halyard, a jug of ale in hand. Toby told him of the boat he had seen for sale which was now shored up along the bay waiting to be cleaned. Taking advantage of the low tide, they wasted no time and headed off to inspect the vessel.

The Dunstan was shored up at the far end of the harbour, opposite the north wall of the prison. Seeing her out of the water, the fluyt was an ungainly sight. Twice the girth of any other vessel of the same length, the boat looked like a beached walrus: a veteran sea-cow tired of her days at sea. Having little options open to them, both men continued their inspection of the boat.

Considering her age, the hull was in remarkably good condition and, once the planks had been cleared of barnacles, there would be little work to be done. One thing in her favour was the decoration at the stern – two porpoises beautifully carved into the taffrail at each side of the nameplate. Whoever had built the vessel had given particular attention to the ornamentation and the feature gave some encouragement to the two entrepreneurs. John set about pacing the distance from stern to bowsprit: eighty-five feet. They both stood at the head of the beach to check the alignment of masts & rigging: all appeared to be in good order.

"That there your tub, Mister?" The two men looked around but failed to see where the wispy voice came from. They looked towards the prison. Through an opening, high up the wall, a thin face with a long white beard pushed its way through the iron bars. "I'll wager you fifty guineas that as soon as I'm skinny enough to slip through these bars, I'll race you across the bay to Saint Catherine."

From what they could see of the old man, he was little more than skin and bones as it was: hardly much chance of him getting any thinner.

"Give you a head start, that I will," continued the old timer. "In fact, I'll let you set full sails in that bath tub before I start swimming."

The old man did have a point. How much headway would this boat make in a light wind? Should the old dog up on the wall ever make his escape, the fifty-guinea wager he proposed would likely be in his favour. The prisoner continued to rant from his cell as Toby and the Mate climbed the ladder to board the vessel.

It was peaceful on deck now they were out of sight of the prison wall; somewhat strange though to be so high up and surrounded by a sea of golden sands. From their position they had a view across the Palisadoes; a narrow strip of land bordered by mangroves with over a hundred little inlets and bays. It is said that this isthmus is inhabited by sea crocodiles twice the length of a man and, should anyone dare to venture into the area, they are sure to never return.

Toby and John took the opportunity to take a close look around the vessel: ratlines checked for wear and tear, all spars, gaffs and booms inspected, most appeared to be in very good condition. However, the vessel must have been involved in a collision at some stage: John pointed out that some repair was needed to the port scupper and they took a closer look. No sooner had they moved to the rail, the ranting from the prison wall started up again.

"Hey skipper! You looking for a crew for that bucket? I'm an experienced hand."

"What? No you ain't!" The old man was joined by another, two cells further along the wall.

John reminded his captain that, if they were going to take on this vessel, they will have to get a move on and muster the crew together.

"Twenty-five years at sea, I have," continued the old timer.

"You liar, Hooper! You ain't been a day at sea."

"Don't you take no notice of him, captain," the old man continued. "He gone and murdered his mother for sixpence, he did."

"You wait till I get out of here, Hooper. I'm gonna skin you alive!"

"What, like you done to your dear old lady?"

Satisfied that most of the vessel was in good order both entrepreneurs descended the ladder of the Dutch Fluyt. The voices from the grey stone prison wall continued unabated as they headed back along the beach towards town.

The Spar and Halyard offered lodgings at a reasonable price. So, in view of their limited resources, Toby and John decided to share a room at the inn. The accommodation was simple to say the least; two bunk beds, a small table with one chair and an oil lamp on the table for their use. Unfortunately, there was no window which meant the air in the room was stale. However, with the promise of a hearty meal awaiting them they discarded their belongings and returned to the common room.

The food was disappointing; the lamb pie contained far too much mace and wine vinegar, the lamb was exercise for the jaw and tasted suspiciously like horse meat. However, as the meal was included in the fare, they made the best of it and took the opportunity to discuss their new venture.

Toby tried to sound enthusiastic. "The hold will probably take on double that of the Chesapeake."

"Thrice, I'd say, Captain. But how long will she make it to get home?"

Toby rubbed his chin. "Depends on the ballast, I wouldn't care to risk sailing her too high, even if it means we would make good headway."

"Well, don't seem we have much choice, Captain. There ain't no other vessels up for sale."

Toby pushed his half-eaten meal across the table. "So, do we have a deal then?"

"I'm in at four to the ten," said John.

"That's settled then, sixty-forty."

Both men shook hands.

"So, all we need now is to find another four-hundred and fifty escudos." John said.

The two entrepreneurs decided to waste no time and make an offer for the vessel there and then.

They were outside and about to set off to the ship chandler when a man staggered over towards them.

"Beggin' yer pardon, Sirs. But is one o' you a Mister Fowler skipper of the Chesty Beak?"

"The Chesapeake," Toby corrected. "Yes, I'm the Captain."

"And I'm John Fowler," added the Mate.

The man looked from one to the other. He squeezed his eyes tight and gave his head a violent shake. "Well, I think ye should know yer midshipman ain't feelin' too good."

Matthew! Both Toby and John looked to one another.

"Where will we find him?"

"Yer physi. . . physi. . ."

"Physician?" offered Toby.

"That's it! Well, anyways, 'e sent me to tell ye."

"Where are they?" repeated John.

The man swayed a little and stared into the Mate's eyes for a few seconds. "The Spare an' Haggle Hard in Thames Street."

"Spar and Halyard? But that's where we're now!" said John.

The man looked up at the sign above the tavern door then turned back to Toby and John. "Ah, no, that'll where thee be. . . They be top o' Cannon Street next t' meat market."

The Captain and the Mate had already set a good pace along the quayside when the man called after them, demanding a shilling for his trouble.

As luck would have it, despite his confusion, the drunkard had a good memory for directions. They found Matthew Wilkins with his back against the wall of the last building at the north end of Cannon Street. Standing alongside him was Michael Talbert, a close friend of Matthew. However, it was unfortunate that a small gathering had also taken some interest.

John was the first to speak. "How is he, Michael?"

"Just took on one of his turns. We was having a quiet drink in that tavern over there, an' Matthew started complaining of a head pain. Next minute he was talking real strange like."

"How much do you think he's had to drink, Mister Talbert?"

"Hardly nothing at all, Captain. We only just got here about an hour ago."

"With respect, Captain," John intervened. "But this does seem to be one of his usual –"

"Keep thy accusations within thee else I pull out thy tongues and feed them to the cats!"

They all turned to look at Matthew who had both hands pressed to each side of his head. The sound that came from the the boy was not of this earth. And certainly not the voice of Midshipman Wilkins.

"If thy walk this land," the voice continued, "Thy shall be smitten."

The man at the front of the gathering around them turned to his friend. "That boy speaks the truth. This place has the blessing of the Devil."

His friend nodded. "You're right there, Thomas. Makes you think. Don't it."

Matthew shook his head from side to side. "Go hence from this place and return to me what is rightly mine," the voice insisted.

The Mate turned to Toby. He nodded up the street where four females, arms linked, were striding towards them. "Best we get young Matthew away from here, don't you think Captain?"

The women reminded Toby of the strumpet in the cage near the Turtle Market. He spoke to Michael. "Where is Matthew lodging, Mister Talbert?"

"Same as me, Captain. The Duchess of Windsor in Broad Street."

Toby was trying to determine where Broad Street was located when the strumpets turned up and one of them stepped up to Matthew.

"Oh, what ever is the the matter my pretty? You looks like you could do with a little female company." She turned to her companions. "What say you, girls?"

Her friends all agreed.

"Depart from here this instant, else the Master strike thee down," came the voice.

"Huh?" The woman took a step back.

The two men in the gathering who had been following Matthew's words joined in. "Take heed of the prophet's wisdom, Harlot. Come join with us and depart from this wicked place," said one. "He has a good point there, ladies," said the other.

The woman stared at the two men in disbelief. "I wouldn't go with you two pissy weasels if you paid me double!" She pushed through the crowd to join her friends. "Come on girls, we're wasting our time here."

Toby, John and Michael waited until the quartet disappeared around the corner of High Street then, with Matthew at their side, they took the same route. For much of the journey they were followed by Matthew's disciples and it wasn't until they reached *The Duchess of Windsor* that a few could be persuaded to disperse. As for the remainder, they refused to leave until they were presented with a shilling.

Once they had installed the boy at his lodgings his maladies vanished, as did his strange way of speech. When asked what he meant by it all, Matthew couldn't recall anything.

Time was moving on. Whilst Toby and John had planned to visit the chandler and make an offer for the Fluyt, they were concerned about the events of the past hour and asked that Michael Talbert stay with Matthew for the remainder of the day.

A price was agreed at the chandlers on condition that the scupper would be repaired and the careening would be completed by the middle of the month. Apart from raising the extra finance, all that remained to be done was to find the crew of the Chesapeake and arrange them to muster at the dock on the third Wednesday of the month.

This proved to be more difficult than planned: Out of the eleven survivors, only seven wished to make the return journey home. Both Daniel Fish and Michael Stroud had been seduced by the profit that could be made from piracy and had already signed up for raids on the coast of Cartengena. Isaac Jacobs had already left for Barbados where he had originally intended to settle, and Marcus Dodds was in jail for killing an officer of the militia during a brawl. Although Nathaniel Lathan would be returning to his home in Boston, with the loss of his right arm, his duties as a deck hand would be restricted. So, in addition to Toby and John, that left only six able-bodied men; Henry Jackson, Matthew Wilkins, Samuel Taponket, Robert Davies, Michael Talbert and Joseph Freeman.

Even a vessel such as the Dunstan would need a crew of at least twelve to be seaworthy. The only option was to recruit more hands. The word was passed around that the Dunstan would be bound for the colonies of Virginia and Maryland, and the Captain and Mate would be recruiting able seamen at the Spar and Halyard.

That evening at the inn, Toby and John booked a private room especially for the occasion of interviews. All the necessary documents were neatly arranged and laid out on a table which they pulled over to the wall to allow ample space for a queue to form from the common room. At the appointed hour of eight, both men squeezed onto the bench betwixt the table and the wall and waited for the recruits. At half of the hour past eight, no-one had yet arrived. Convinced that they had set the time too early, they refreshed themselves with another jug of ale.

"Did you call on Matthew?" Toby asked.

"Aye. In the last hour. He seems fine. Head pains gone. No strange talk. As fit as the day he signed on."

"The way of his speaking was much the same as that Watts girl in Plymouth, don't you think?"

"T'was strange indeed, Captain."

"I wish now I had not taken him with me. I thought nothing good would come of it."

"I believe it's the witch who's more the cause of it, Captain."

"Do you really believe in all that nonsense, John? If you had observed the old woman for yourself, you would have seen she was without malice. Yet another victim of witchcraft fury in that colony. The poor woman had dispute with her neighbours, that was all. All the talk of spells and magical powers was just an excuse to claim a piece of land that was rightfully hers."

"Did you not tell me that your friend, the Minister, had been taken ill soon after all this?"

"Did I say that?"

"You said you received a letter from your fiancée."

"She's not my fiancée."

"Lady friend, then."

With all the distractions over the last few days he'd forgotten about Sarah's letter. Toby made a point to send a reply before leaving Port Royal.

"Yes, that as may be," said Toby. "But the Reverend Eastman's duties had made particular demands on his health at the time and the exorcism would have sapped his spirit. I would say these were more likely to be the reason for his illness." While Toby had considered that the Minister's declining heath may have been caused by his connection with the Widow Hobbs, he was reluctant to admit it.

"And wasn't young Matthew taken with his strange doings soon after you took him to call on the old widow?"

Toby now wished he hadn't brought up the subject. He felt guilty enough about his involvement with Nathaniel Eastman's business. While he may have been ready and willing to help the Minister with his task, he was beginning to realise his participation may have made things worse. And now the Mate was making the connection between these events and Matthew: as if Toby didn't know.

"Very odd," said John.

Toby didn't respond.

"Don't you think it strange, Captain, that the boy is fit an' healthy at all other times?"

"Midshipman Wilkins?"

"Yes, Matthew."

It was to Toby's relief that they were interrupted by their first applicant. A man who was proud to announce he had reached the age of sixty-five came to sit opposite the two entrepreneurs and asked if they would like to purchase a copper wind vane which he believed to be most useful to sailing vessels.

At the hour of eleven, a whore who had seen better days, rested her ample bosom on the table and asked the two gentlemen if she could be considered for recruitment. Her name was Sally and she professed to be very good with her hands. Not only would it be considered bad luck to have a lady on board but, on reflection, and considering the limited number of crew, her distractions may prove to be a hazard to the safety of the voyage. It was decided that her service might be better appointed on a larger more populated vessel. Once Sally had departed from their company, Toby and his business partner collected up the papers, which had by then littered the floor, and retired for the night.

Saturday was much the same, and so was Sunday. On Monday they cancelled the booking of the private room, and instead arranged to meet for one hour in the common room: Still no recruits.

It was not until the Tuesday that an able seaman by the name of William Burnley, a man who had spent too many years in the Caribbean and wished to return to his home in Virginia, approached their table. The man was fair, a few inches taller than Toby and most importantly, he appeared to be strong and healthy: certainly capable of handling most of the tasks required of a deck hand. Burnley was respectful during the interview and struck up a good rapport with the Mate. He was immediately taken on.

All was quiet after the man had left.

John broke the silence. "Things seem to be looking up, eh Captain?" He raised his tankard as a toast to their success.

But Toby was distracted. Eventually, he picked up his ale and took a sip. "Do you think we may have been a little hasty?" he ventured. "After all, we know very little about this man."

"Burnley? Seems fine to me."

"Yes, but we didn't even ask what he has been doing here in Port Royal. For all we know, he might be up to anything."

Until that date, Toby had been particularly careful in his choice of crew; usually a hand who he had known for some time and proved to be of good character. This was the first time he had taken on a stranger. "What if he's on the run? Didn't he say he was in a hurry to get away from here?"

John sighed. "Aren't we all, Captain?"

The two sat in silence until John finished his drink.

"Well, I think the man be fine. He comes across like a good sort of fellow, I'd say."

"Oh yes, that's another thing. I didn't like the way he was trying to gain your favour, John. It was as if he wanted to be your friend."

"Ah, so that's what's got under your jib."

"What do you mean?"

The Mate gave Toby a sideways look. "Your concern, Captain, is that this new recruit may fit well with our crew, and that would leave you. . ."

"Leave me, what?"

John looked down and stared into his empty tankard.

"Come on, Mister Fowler, say it," Toby pressed.

John looked up from the table. "With respect, Captain, it would do you no harm if, once in a while, you was to share some time with your crew."

"What do you suggest? Get drunk and go whoring?" Toby could feel his blood temperature rise.

"No, not that. Just talk to them sometimes."

"I do talk to them," Toby objected.

"Yes, but I mean in a social way. Not just give 'em orders."

"Oh, I see. So, instead of giving the order to set the topsail, you suggest that I just sit around with my crew and converse on the general topic of the day, is that it? I'm sure that'll gain me respect."

John let out an exasperated sigh and rested his chin in his hands. "You already have their respect, Captain." His eye fixed on the flickering flame of an oil lamp which hung from the beam at the entrance of the tavern. "I'm meeting up with a few of the crew this evening, why don't you come along?" John suggested. "They be sure pleased to see you."

"I thank you for your kind offer, John, but I have another engagement," Toby lied. "But please be sure to pass on my appreciation to the others."

The Mate got up from his chair and stretched.

"As you wish, Captain. I'll be seeing you in the morning then."

Toby watched his Mate head toward the door. The nerve of the man! Just because he found it easy to mix with people doesn't give him the right to assume everyone else should be the same. Anyway, what could Toby possibly have in common with his crew?

He finished his drink and, not wishing to stay any longer in the common room, retired to their lodgings.

Chapter 14 – At the Spar and Halyard

Toby set the lamp down on the table in their lodgings, the words of his Mate dominating his thoughts. An implication was hidden within them, he was sure of it: that he was the subject of ridicule amongst his own crew. He could hear them laughing now, probably led by one or two he could name: Davies for one. There was something about that man's manner that hinted at insubordination; always ready with a contradictory remark against his captain's decisions. Davies had made it quite clear from the beginning that his service on the Chesapeake would only be a temporary one until he was in a position to build up his business again. Help a man out of a difficult corner, and that's the gratitude you receive in return.

Toby wished he had some way of escape from these thoughts. He searched his bag and found the essay given to him by Sarah before leaving Boston. He read the title page: *An Essay to Revive the Antient Education of Gentlewomen, in Religion, Manners, Arts and Tongues.*

He was halfway through the second page before he realized that he hadn't taken in a word. Was it usual for the master of a vessel to be on familiar terms with members of his crew? Surely that would be somewhat patronizing and such familiarity could lead to all manner of problems. He turned back to the first page of the document and read again. The introduction outlined the content of the essay: an argument in favour of educating women in the arts and languages so that their relations with menfolk would profit.

He could imagine these sentiments making a great impression on Sarah: a woman of reason amidst men bound by their religious doctrines. He could see her now, standing before the Boston council, trying to convince them with her argument for equality. They would listen to her reasoning, then, after careful consideration, deliver their objection on the grounds that her words would contradict their commitment to *The Compact*. No wonder people were assigning the name *Puritan* to the founders of this colony.

How long had it been since he last saw Sarah? Three months? Nearly four. Toby took out his writing case and set it up on the table. After fifteen minutes he sat back and read through what he had written.

My dearest Sarah. Please forgive the lapse of time since I last set pen to paper and wrote to you, for much has happened since I left Sainte Mary. It is with difficulty that I relate the fate of my wonderful new vessel, the Chesapeake Venture. After spending ten days in James Town, we set sail for Barbadoes and, with the aide of north-easterlies, made very good headway. That vessel in which, as you know, I had placed all my savings, lived up to all my expectations. I use the past tense here, for on the fifth day of our journey we were taken by a pirate sloop. Try as we did to outrun her, the Chesapeake was no match for this heavily-armed vessel. As God is my witness, the only option was to hand over the ship to these barbarians in order to spare the lives of my crew. As I write this account, I perceive it a miracle that God has preserved us, for the taking of our vessel was only the beginning of our tribulations.

But before I give account of my own adventures, I must tell you that my thoughts have been with you and I am eager to discover how you fared with your meeting with the elders in Boston. I have this very moment the paper by Bathsua Makin that you gave me and consider it to be an eloquent proposal. If you are planning to refer to it in your debate, may I suggest that you avoid mention of educated Grecian or Roman ladies but instead focus attention on learned women quoted in the Scriptures, particularly the fact that Miriam was a great poet and philosopher. I would also think it unwise to give the argument taken by Makin which suggest that educated ladies would shame men of their ignorance, for this will only rouse the heckles of your audience. . . Some good news. I have acquired a new vessel. Although somewhat modest in comparison to the Chesapeake, it will be enough to get us home. We plan, should all go well, to sail within the next week and set a course for Sainte Mary passing through Virginia.

There had been much talk of recent Indian troubles pervading the Plymouth Colony and Toby was considering how he could address his concern of this to Sarah when his thoughts were interrupted by the sound of a key turning in the lock of his door.

John was surprised to see Toby seated at the table of their lodgings. "I thought you had an appointment, Captain?"

"Oh, that. It was postponed to a later date," Toby lied. "And what of your own social engagement with the crew? Nobody turn up?"

"On the contrary, Captain. They are waiting for me down in the common room. I just came up to collect this." John held up his purse. He seemed to be about to add something more but Toby turned back to his writing. When the Mate had gone he gave a cursory glance towards the closed door, shook his head and returned his attention to the letter. He re-read what he had written so far.

There was no mention of the casualties occurring during the Chesapeake's misadventures and Toby considered whether he should include this in his letter. Would the families of those unfortunate victims be expecting news of their loved ones by now?

He considered who they had they lost since leaving for Barbados; Edmund Browne who, soon after leaving Virginia, had fallen overboard after a heavy bout of drinking. William Carter who was buried at sea after procuring a fatal illness. Then at Tortuga; John Coote, now presumed dead after attempting to escape to the woods, and William Foster, shot in a pistol duel after being forced to settle a gambling dispute with a pirate. That left those who suffered fatal injury during battle at Maracaibo; Owen Fuller; decapitated by a canon ball, and Adam Milward who had the misfortune to be in the storeroom when it was blown up by a grenade. John Butcher, Simon Croft and Richard Hobson were all drowned at sea while attempting to swim to the rescuing vessel at Maracaibo bar. Toby tried not to think of the sharks awaiting their arrival. Toby decided it would be better not to mention these casualties in his letter to Sarah as she may see it as her responsibility to inform the families of those who lived in Plymouth. He tried to recall the content of her previous letter. Was it there that she wrote of Nathaniel's ill health? Toby took up the quill.

I was concerned to read in your letter that Nathaniel Eastman has been unwell. Please give him my regards and tell him he is in my prayers. I did not have the occasion to tell you of my last visit to the Minister's house, as we departed for Sainte Mary before I had chance to see you. It so happen that the Minister asked for my opinion of a girl who was in his care and who had been taken by some demonic possession. Nathaniel was particularly affected by the activities of the girl in question and I do hope all has resolved itself for the better.

Toby felt he was partly to blame for the Nathaniel's condition. The Minister had asked him to investigate the old widow who was presumed to be the cause of the girl's manifestations. Despite having witnessed some very strange phenomena performed by the Watts girl, Toby had still remained somewhat cynical – yet another example of his error of judgement. If only he could step back in time and put things right. Had Toby not been so dismissive of the power Widow Hobbs had over the Watts girl then the Minister may have taken more care when dealing with the case. Also, when the woman asked who sent Toby to investigate, he now wished he had not been so hasty in giving the Minister's name. At the time, he concluded that the widow was just another innocent victim of witchcraft accusations. How wrong he was.

It seems obvious now that Widow Hobbs did have *a gift*, as she called it; for how could she possibly have known Toby's father lived in Jamaica? It also appears that she may have had far more to do with the Watts case than Toby had at first surmised: her motive being revenge against her neighbours.

Distracted as he was with these thoughts, Toby hadn't taken note of the time. There was a sloop bound for Boston in the morn and, if he was to send the letter, he would need to finish it before John returned.

While it was convenient, and made financial sense, for him to share accommodation with Mr Fowler, there were some disadvantages. John was a social type and, although Toby was not averse to occasional discourse, there were times when the Mate's incessant talk became obtrusive. There was also the matter of snoring. Since Toby had agreed to share a room at the Spar and Halyard, he had not had one night of uninterrupted rest: the noise emitting from the man's throat was liken to the sound of a coach and horses racing through cobbled streets of the town. And of course there was the smoking; a disgusting habit at the best of times, but here the accommodation was without natural ventilation and whenever Fowler set a light to his pipe the tiny room was taken over by the acrid stench. The only hope for Toby was to ensure he got his head down well before John Fowler returned. Then there was a chance he could drift off and be oblivious to the man's habits. No sooner had he finished his letter to Sarah, the door swung open.

"Evenin', Captain. Didn't expect to see you up an' about." John swaggered across the room and slumped onto the corner of his bunk. "What a night! You should 'ave come. We all started out at that place in New Street." He pulled out his pipe and set it alight.

One hour later Toby was lying in his bunk staring up at the smoke filled ceiling. He counted the snores and reached one hundred and fifteen before the dark veil of sleep took him away to a place he preferred not to be.

Chapter 15 – Three Blinde Mice

The following morning it was decided that, should they not be able to recruit any more hands by the end of that day, they will delay the muster date by another week. Should that fail to procure the required number, Toby and John both agreed they would abandon the project altogether.

Later that same afternoon, despite this agreement, they put their trust in fate and kept their appointment at the harbour office.

The official was a thin man with a pointed chin and an equally pointed nose. His lank hair, hanging thick to his shoulders, was thinning on top: the few strands brushed across the pinnacle of his cranium did little to disguise this fact. The man, who reminded Toby of a bilge rat, looked up from his important papers at the two men standing before his desk. Without a word, he held out his hand and took a cursory glance at the vessel's registration document.

"Tonnage?" the man didn't even look up.

"Two hundred and fifteen," Toby replied.

"Load?"

Both Toby and John looked at each other quizzically.

The man behind the desk sighed. "What cargo do you propose to load here in Port Royal?"

"Oh, sugar and general victuals." Toby replied.

"General victuals?" the official looked at the two with an air of contempt. "Can you be more specific?"

Toby was beginning to be irritated with the little man. "How can I possibly know that at this stage? The boat is still beached up for careening."

John quickly stepped forward. "What the captain is saying, Sir, is the victuals be the personal effects of the crew. If you please. . . Sir."

The official considered this for a moment. "Then I suggest, Gentlemen. You make an appointment at this office once you have decided the nature of cargo you intend to load into your vessel. Shall we say. . . " He opened a journal on his desk. "Five weeks from Monday next?" He looked from one to the other with a smug expression.

At that moment, a clerk, his features half-hidden under an untidy wig, entered the room and placed a pile of papers on the desk. The clerk gave Toby a nod and left without saying a word.

The official gave a fleeting look at the pile and studied the two men. "Let's get on with this. Date of sailing?" He seemed to have overlooked his previous decision.

"That all depends on how long –"

"Thursday the sixteenth," John interrupted.

"Sign here, please." He spun the document around and passed the quill over to the Mate.

"That'll be twenty-six pounds gentlemen, please."

Few words passed between John and Toby as they left the harbour office. The duty had to be paid in advance whether they purchased the vessel or not: monies they had not accounted for.

Downhearted, the pair made their way back to their lodgings at the *Spar and Halyard* tavern. Half-way down Queen Street, they passed an inn which promised a good meal at a reasonable price. Not wishing to experience another of the Halyard's meat pies, they stepped inside and sat down to a plate of turtle stew and rice which, as it happened, was delightful. Their stomachs replenished, the Captain and Mate of the Dunstan were consoled.

A party arrived at the inn and took position at a table nearby. The group wished to make it known to all that they had recently arrived in Port Royal after weeks at sea and were looking for sport in town. Their bellies filled with rum, the rowdy group soon began to pester the customers in the room; one in particular became the focus of their attention. Seated at the next table was a man who made the grave mistake of asking the party to tone down their noise. Their response was to invite him to join them for a share of their drink. There was, however, an obligation on the part of their guest. After each shot of rum taken, the man was ordered to dance the boards while his hosts used his feet as a target for their knives. Adapting their own words to the tune of a children's rhyme, they each took a turn to throw.

"One poor sod, one poor sod, see how he dance, see how he dance," the blood-thirsty band chanted as their victim leapt high in the air to avoid the next throw. The hum of a blade rang out over the words as it struck home into the boards an inch from the poor man's toes. The victim's cries for mercy were lost over the chanting of the band around him. Of course, the proprietor was nowhere to be seen and the man's only consolation was the occasional break to down another drink before the cruel game resumed.

John turned to Toby. "We best find Davies, don't you think, Captain?"

"Yes, I suppose we should."

While Toby didn't relish the thought of spending any time with Davies, the alternative was to have a dispute with a bunch of pirates.

"Do you know where he is likely to be?" Toby asked, secretly hoping John didn't.

"Aye, I have an idea."

While the buccaneers were occupied with their sport, Toby and John slipped away unnoticed.

At the western end of the town, near to Fisher's Row and hidden away between a warehouse and a cobbler, was a tobacco trader. A door opened directly onto the street and led down three steps into a shop which, in addition to the sale of *the best tobacco in the colonies*, also traded as a wine merchant. Like most of the shops in town, there was opportunity to stay and sample the goods on offer. With John's purchase of a quarter of Virginia Tobacco, he and Toby armed themselves each with a glass of fine French brandy and waited for the Chesapeake's purser to turn up.

Davies eventually appeared from the back of the shop. He picked up the Mate's purchase and took a sniff. "You can do better than this, John."

After taking off with the bag, he returned a minute later with another. "This one is grown in Hispaniola, and cured in the shade away from the sun. You try it. Tell me what you think."

Back in Maryland, on completion of his indenture, Davies had been given a plot of fifty acres on high ground in Somerset County. With the help of Yaocomico Indians, he cultivated this plot over several seasons and soon became the most successful tobacco grower in the parish. Toby had supplied the trading link with Davies and very quickly his blend of weed was in demand along the tidewater settlements. Then disaster struck: During the disputes with the Susquehannock Indians, Davies' farm was burnt to the ground and his crop completely ruined. With no funds to start again, Toby had taken him on as purser which, with his bartering skills, had proved to be very profitable for trade.

But Davies' first love was cultivating tobacco and it was not certain how long he would remain at sea. As John had a good rapport with the man, Toby left his Mate to see if he was willing to sign on.

"We sail on the Wednesday next," said John.

"Hmm. . . You calling in anywhere on the voyage?"

The Mate looked to Toby for an answer.

"James Town."

"Which one would that be?" Davies asked.

"James Town Virginia, and one or two places to take on fresh supplies and water."

"All right, I'm with you, but I would care to reserve a space in the hold for my own trade."

"How much?" said John.

"About forty cubits square."

The Mate checked for his captain's approval.

Leaving John to arrange the details Toby decided to purchase a flask of the brandy he had sampled. As he waited at the counter, a small party of customers stepped down into the shop; two well attired gentleman accompanied by their ladies. One of the group moved in alongside Toby.

"Hello my sweet Tobias. I hope you have been rehearsing your steps of the Sarabande."

Toby spun round to face Elizabeth.

"Oh, er, yes. I mean no, not yet." The recollection of that night at the rooms of Lord Rumsay came flooding back.

Did you find my note?"

"Yes I did. Thank you."

"Then you should arrange another lesson with me sometime. How long are you intending to stay here?"

"Oh, I am only here to sign on hands for our new vessel." Toby gave a furtive glance towards the two men watching him from the bench.

"A new vessel? How fascinating. So you are planning to leave Port Royal soon?"

"A little more complicated than that, I fear." Toby shuffled his feet uneasily. He was irritated on two counts; firstly he was uncomfortable with the line of questioning pursued by Elizabeth and, secondly, by the fact John Fowler had appeared at the counter with the obvious intention of listening to their converse.

"Complications?" Elizabeth asked.

"Oh, it is just a financial matter." Toby was reminded of how he had been misled by this very woman. "It appears that this town is only concerned with extracting a fee for every turn." He shot Elizabeth a disapproving look.

She ignored this. "You are seeking to raise funds for your venture?"

"Yes, but –"

"I may be able to help. How much finance do you need?"

So amused was Toby by this last comment that it was with some difficulty that he was able to contain himself. "Well, I thank you for your offer." Toby pulled himself together. "But we need something in the region of five hundred escudos. I am certain we can find a benefactor before long."

"Well, if not, you know how to find me," said Elizabeth. "Have you perchance seen Beatrice since our evening together?"

"No, I haven't." Toby felt the colour rise to his cheeks. He could sense the Mate propped up alongside them.

"Nor I." Elizabeth was obviously concerned. "We left you in the early hours. At two or thereabouts, and I have not seen nor heard from her since."

Toby cleared his throat. He nodded towards the door where Elizabeth's companions, bottles in hand, were preparing to leave the shop. "I should not detain you any longer."

She signalled for them to wait. "One thing before I go," she said. "There was a gentleman enquiring about you."

"Yes, as I said, I have been enlisting a new crew."

"This was the morning after our meeting."

"What did you tell him?"

"I did not care for the man. I said that I knew not of your whereabouts."

Elizabeth's companions were now calling to her from the door.

"I have to go, Toby. I hope we meet again soon."

As the group stepped out into the street, Elizabeth turned to blow him a kiss.

Toby picked up the flask on the counter in such haste that the bottle almost slipped from his fingers. He studied the label and looked up to the proprietor. "Yes, this will be fine." He pulled out his purse.

"Well, that's a turn up, Captain. I'm impressed!"

"Oh, yes, well." He held up the flask. "It's only a bottle of brandy, John."

The Mate raised his eyes to the heavens. "You know I'm not speaking of that. I'm talking of the lady."

"Oh, that. She is just a passing acquaintance."

"More than that, I wager. Didn't she just offer to help solve our problems?"

"Oh, yes. But I doubt she is in a position to raise –"

"Forgive me, Captain, but some of the whores in this town are amongst the richest womenfolk in the colonies."

"Whores?" Toby was furious. "What makes you think she is a whore?"

The Mate let out a sigh. "That's fine, Captain. Let's leave it at that."

"But you cannot make a statement like that and just let it go."

John Fowler turned and headed back to the bench. The remainder of the room was quiet; all eyes were on Toby as he joined his companions.

Once the captain had calmed down John ventured to pursue the subject. "No matter who she is, Captain, does it not make sense to follow up her offer?"

"She was just making an impression. I really don't think her suggestion was serious."

"Sounded serious to me."

"Well, not I" Toby picked up his glass. "Look, can we close this topic now?"

"As you wish, Captain."

Davies had been sitting alongside them in silence. "Before you do dismiss the subject, Gentlemen, one thing which may be worth your consideration." He glanced at Toby. "If the lady is as well acquainted with our Master as all appearances suggest."

Toby was about to explode.

"And if she is of the profession you imply," Davies quickly continued. "Then you may have made a most valuable acquaintance indeed." Davies looked at his two companions. "She will certainly have her finger on the pulse of some of the best contacts in town."

Apart from a few subtle references, nothing further was said on the subject that evening.

That night, to the accompaniment of the Mate's snores, Toby thought of his chance meeting with Elizabeth and how humiliating it was to be witnessed by Fowler and Davies. The remarks and innuendoes from both were too much to bear. How could they think he would consider setting up a financial association with a woman like her? And it wasn't the fact she is a whore. That had nothing to do with it. No, the only reason Toby was reluctant to get involved with Elizabeth was that she had deceived him. If she and Beatrice had made it clear from the beginning what their motives were that night, then his feelings about them would have been different. But he couldn't place the blame on Beatrice to the same degree. After all, she was not the instigator of their amusements that evening; it was Elizabeth. Was is not she who approached Toby at his table? And was it not Elizabeth who suggested they continue their diversions in the private rooms of

Lord Rumsay? And what of the games? The invitation to dance? Were any of these instigated by Beatrice? Certainly not! All were part of a ruse devised only by Elizabeth.

But what were her motives? What possible reason could Elizabeth want to get involved with Toby? What sort of catch was he? A captain without a ship, an adventurer with little resources, a man with no future prospects. And why was she so keen to bring Beatrice into her scheme? Toby was perplexed. What of the chance meeting that evening? Why bring Beatrice into the conversation? Could it be that Elizabeth knew it would embarrass him? At this very moment she and Beatrice were probably laughing at the recount of that meeting.

Toby tried to direct his thoughts to the other matters of the day. They had now enlisted a total of seven hands and they were still a long way off the mark. He remembered the poor man at the hand of the pirates; the irony of hearing an innocent children's song adapted to accompany such a cruel act and felt a touch of shame at not being able to rescue him. He remembered that tune from his childhood. The words came back to him just as sleep arrived to take him away to that distant past.

Three blinde mice, three blinde mice – Toby sat up in his bunk. The letter from his father! That was the rhyme to which he was referring! He must return to La Bruma tomorrow.

Chapter 16 – A Tranquil Setting

After spending nearly a week in Port Royal it was refreshing to step off the jetty and take a brisk walk up to St Jago. Toby had procured a passage on the earliest water-boat that morning which meant that the streets of the old Spanish town were almost empty. He took a deep breath and filled his lungs with the sweet scent of hibiscus and geraniums: nothing like the stench of the crammed streets he had left behind. Even the buildings in the centre of town, fashioned in the Spanish style, allowed sufficient space to breathe. After the night's rain, the warm rays of the morning sun touched the road ahead, releasing a gentle mist from the cobbles.

Leaving the town to the south, the walk was particularly pleasant with no-one to distract him. As the road began its gentle climb, each bend offered a different perspective. The eastern part of the bay was bordered by golden sands. Looking back to the south, he was presented with a wonderful view of Spanish Town with its central square and administrative buildings. Even the distant peninsula of Palisadoes, crammed with the houses of Port Royal, seemed to take on an attractive spirit. Toby tried to find his new vessel, but it was difficult enough to identify the larger ships at this distance. The ocean beyond the peninsula was as smooth as a looking-glass and the horizon no more than a gentle cloud of mist blending sky with sea.

The vegetation on the slopes to each side of the track had been cleared to make way for fields of sugar cane, some already harvested, some awaiting the cut. At the next bend, a cart pulled over to the side of the road. A team of Negroes, machetes in hand, descended from the cart and silently spaced themselves along the barricade of cane that towered the edge of the roadside. While Toby was prepared to raise his hat to greet them, none lifted their eyes from the ground and all were silent as he passed them by.

The track hugged the field where the workers had started their cutting then disappeared sharply at the next crest of the hill. Once Toby rounded this bend, he came in sight of his father's farm. The road curved for a good half-mile before it met the house; a steep valley, rich in wild vegetation, separated him from the property. The line of trees leading up to the front porch of the house cast long shadows across the carriageway. To the left and a little further up the slope, there were some more outbuildings which Toby hadn't noticed on his first visit. The sun was high enough now to light up the east side of the property and the hill beyond was touched with a thin layer of mist: a scene presenting a magical picture of *La Bruma*.

Stopping to take in a new angle whenever the view permitted, it took a good while before Toby reached the gates of the house. As soon as he turned into the carriageway, there was the familiar grating sound and the front door flung open. Eduardo jumped down the steps and ran forwards to greet him. Within three paces of Toby, the boy came to a sudden halt. He looked sheepishly at the ground, as if uncertain of his next move.

"Good morning, Eduardo – Como estas?" Toby reached out to shake the boy's hand.

"Good mornin', Mister Toby," the boy announced in English. He beamed.

"Is your mother in the house?"

Eduardo looked puzzled. Toby repeated the question in Spanish. He now wished that he had brought the boy a present.

"Si, si, ella esta en casa!" (She's at home!) Eduardo thought for a moment, then smiled. "Les go!" making a signal for Toby to follow.

In the kitchen Magdalena was standing at her usual position at the worktop slicing some chunks from a huge melon. On the table was his father's box. Toby pondered the reason it should be here when, on his previous visit, he remembered leaving it in his father's study.

"You take long time getting up here," she said, her eyes fixed on the task. She gave her son a slice and placed another on the table in front of their guest.

Toby hesitated to pick it up. "Well yes, it's a fine morning. I wanted to have a good look around."

"Go on," she insisted, nodding towards the fruit. "It for you."

"Thank you. This is very generous of you."

Magdalena chuckled.

Toby wondered how she knew he was coming up there. "Have you heard from Beatrice?"

"No, not for a week past."

They were silent for a while, each occupied with eating the succulent fruit.

Magdalena was the first to speak. "What you back here for?"

"Oh, yes. I was hoping to collect this." He nodded to the box on the table.

"That all? You not want to stay here?"

"Well yes, but I don't want to inconvenience you. I –"

Magdalena doubled up with laughter. "Oh Lord. The way you talk boy!"

Toby's face was glowing. The laughter continued as Magdalena dragged her slippers across the floor towards the passage. He was lost for words and could only scowl at the woman as she disappeared into the hall. How dare she speak to him like that! Free she may be, but she was still a Negro. And just because she had given birth to his father's child doesn't give her the right to be so familiar; certainly not to humiliate him in that way. He felt a tug on his shirt sleeve.

Eduardo was standing alongside. He held up the model ship. "You play?"

Toby pulled out another chair and the boy sat down next to him. They moved the pewter plate filled with fruit to the edge of the table and were soon set sail from here, heading out across the seas. In less than half a minute they arrived at Toby's box: the shores of England.

"England, England," Eduardo chanted as he moved the model Brig alongside.

The boy wanted to know everything about the strange country hundreds of miles across the ocean; How big were the towns? Does it rain all day? Do they live in big plantations? So many questions.

"Il y a escuela?"

"Yes, some go to school. Some have tutors at home."

Magdalena appeared. "Edo, ven'ca." She lifted the boy down from the chair and turned to Toby. "We go out back."

He gave her a glance, reproaching himself for the harsh opinions he had directed towards her earlier. Why he should feel so guilty, he could not reason.

Once they had left the kitchen, he took the letter from the box and opened it out onto the table. He studied the code at the bottom of the page and wished he had brought a quill and paper. Nevertheless, he attempted the first few letters. Would his assumption prove to be correct?

aI3eIII3a4,eIII3bII3b2cI4

He thought of the beginning of the rhyme; *Three blinde mice, Three blinde mice, Dame Iulian. . .* The first letter would be R, the second D, the third letter of the code was curious because it didn't indicate which word it should come from. Toby carried on with the next few letters which turned out as D, I, another curious code, then E.

So far the first word was – RD?DI?E? That didn't make any sense. Toby was disappointed. The whole purpose for coming all the way up here had been a complete waste of time. He sat with his elbows on the table, head in his hands. Then it came to him. He remembered two things; first that the Roman number in the sequence indicated how many words to skip in each line, also, every third letter of the puzzle would be found following the letter x at the end of the code. He tried again. First letter I, second S, then L, E. The first word was ISLE! Promising. He tried the second. It came out as ST. Isle St. Toby needed to write this down. He folded the letter, returned it to the box, and stepped outside to find Magdalena and the boy.

It took a good while to climb the field behind the villa. Ripened cane, dry and brittle, littered his path as he stumbled up the hillside to find them. Eventually he spotted Magdalena standing in a dense thicket of leafy plants which, at first, Toby had mistaken for banana trees. By the time he reached the top, he didn't care what they were. Soaked in sweat and exhausted, he slumped under the cool leaves only too pleased to escape the mid-morning sun. He looked back across the field. "Why has all this been left to fallow? All the land here –"

"Come." Eduardo's mother was a few feet off the ground testing her weight on a thick branch of a tree. "You come, catch this." She pointed her machete at a bunch of elongated yellow pods, each a little larger then a grapefruit.

Toby got to his feet and stood beside her. The dried scab along his right arm pulled at his skin as he reached up and cupped his hands under the fruit suspended precariously above his head. With a silent swipe of her blade, Toby felt the full weight of the pods. He dropped his arms and held them to his chest.

"You is weak, boy," the woman chuckled as she climbed down. She held out her hand to take them.

Her palm, pale against dark brown skin of her arm, was an open invitation. He'd teach the woman to be so condescending! Toby took a step forward, pushed his chest forward and heaved the heavy fruit into her hand. To his amazement the woman took the whole weight without the slightest effort. Letting out another chuckle, she placed one of the pods into the fork of a fallen branch. One swipe with the blade and the fruit split clean down the middle and fell open to the ground.

The woman sank her hand into the creamy white centre of the fruit and scraped out a bunch of sticky seeds the size of chestnuts. "You know what is this?" she asked.

Toby didn't, and neither did he care.

"Cocoa," she said. "All this is cocoa trees." She made a sweeping gesture to the overgrown tangle of dark green that bordered the field down to the roadside. "You ask why I not make good all this?" She gave Toby a long hard look. "Well I tell you, I ain't to do nothing with it, that why!" There was a note of bitterness to her voice. "Since Mister Edward taken from me, they say I ain't to work this land. It ain't my land and it ain't nobody's to work." The woman shook her head and started off down the hill. "Such waste. Lord, such waste."

Toby followed in silence as Magdalena plodded down a narrow path that bordered the field. Her muttering continued, now accompanied by a sucking through her teeth, until they reached the outbuildings which strung out from the side of the house.

"Mister Toby, Mister Toby! Ven'ca!" Eduardo was running from one of the buildings. He beckoned Toby to follow him inside, but Magdalena caught the boy by the arm and ordered him to fetch the little cart from the storeroom.

"Aw, Mama!" he pleaded.

The woman gave Eduardo a look which sent him slouching off into the shadows of one of the buildings. A minute later he appeared with an old wooden hand cart. The boy slumped down on the base board and began kicking at the dust with his bare heels. When his mother returned, she said nothing to either of them; just tossed two machetes into the cart and marched right back up the hill.

Taking one handle each and keeping their distance from the woman, Toby and the boy pulled the rickety old cart up the steep track. With an occasional nod towards his mother, Eduardo gave a wink and made a circular motion with his finger at the side of his head. Uncertain whether Toby should join forces with his half-brother, he resisted the temptation to laugh.

For the remainder of the morning the three continued to harvest the cocoa pods until the cart was full. It was mid-day before they finished. The dry baked earth scorched the soles of their feet as they made their way back down the hill.

Only when they were back at the house and seated at the kitchen table Magdalena spoke again. "I think you come sell this to the Surinamese."

"Surinamese?"

"Them what comes from Surinam. You not know?" Magdalena frowned, deep furrows cutting into her fleshy brow. "Many come to Jamaica this year. Them all is lookin' for land to grow cane. Three times last month they come up here askin' how much I wanna sell this place." Magdalena took another deep breath, her bosom filling like a foresail. She got up and stood by the window. "That why you come here." The sun was burning down onto the field outside. "I know you gonna sell this land to them."

"I have no intention of selling this place," Toby said.

Magdalena turned to look at him accusingly. "Then, why you here?"

"I came back to have another look at my father's letter." Toby folded his arms. "I know nothing of these Surinamese." He set his lips tight. Why should he have to explain himself to this woman? Compared to many of her kind, she had an easy time of it. If it weren't for setting herself up with his father and getting herself into his bed, she would be working the fields just like the Negroes he had passed that morning. No wonder the woman was concerned.

Magdalena pulled out a chair. "You not like it here?"

"Jamaica? It's very beautiful."

"No, no Lord," she wagged her finger in the air. "Here, this house."

"Oh, yes. It's very pleasant." He could think of a few improvements that could be made but thought it better not to mention them at this time.

Magdalena rested her hands down on the table. "Then why you not take it?"

But she had him wrong. He had no intention of doing anything with the place. Nine acres of neglected hillside and a house in ruins; hardly much of a prospect. If this woman was so keen to continue living here, she was welcome to it. "But this is your home," he said.

Magdalena sucked impatiently through her teeth. She took a deep breath. "I already say to you, they not let me work this land until the papers is signed."

Toby took a while to think about this. It appeared that, unless he made a claim on the title deed, the property will continue to be neglected. He considered the advantage. "If the property is legally mine, would you be willing to manage it?" he asked.

The woman got up and busied herself at the workbench. She placed two cups of molasses water on the table. "And you pay me half of harvest takings?"

"A third."

Magdalena looked up to the window. "A third. But you give me four good men to work the field," she said.

"Agreed."

"Tomorrow we go to office in Santiago?"

"Santiago?" Toby was confused, then he remembered. "Oh, St Jago."

"Yes, Spanish Town. To sign papers."

"Yes, that's fine."

They were about to shake hands when Eduardo bounded into the kitchen. He beamed at his half-brother and mother sitting together at the table. "Mister Toby, ahora, ven'ca! – you come!"

The boy took Toby's arm and led him to one of the outbuildings adjacent to the main house.

In the centre of the floor stood a long stone-built trough covered by a metal grid. Resting along the top of the grid was a row of copper vats, each diminishing in size from a huge container at the far end to the last about the size of a hogshead. Here, the trough extended a further six feet with a narrow opening and was covered with a heavy metal sheet. Eduardo dragged off the cover which fell to the floor with a thud. He reached inside the dark pit and tugged on a piece of flax.

Toby waited patiently. What he saw next caused him to jump. He took a quick step back and almost fell against a pile of logs. There, at the entrance of the tunnel, its fiery mouth agape and its wings spread, was a dragon. That was the only way to describe the creature which stood guard at the entrance of its lair. And if it had not been for the twine secured around the beast's neck, Toby would have bolted for the field.

Eduardo gave another tug on the flax. The creature dug its claws into the ground. The boy reached down. The dragon hissed.

Toby took a step forward. "Careful! What are you doing?" he warned.

But it was too late. The boy had the creature by the neck and was now pulling it towards him. "Ven'ca, Leona." The boy spoke in comforting tones as the animal clawed and twisted in his arms. He then took the creature out into the sunlight. Toby followed at a safe distance.

In the daylight, resting peacefully on the ground, the creature looked far less formidable. It was just under a cubit in length from its head to tail and covered in grey green scales. The boy tied the end of the twine to the handle of the cart and left Toby in its care. Each keeping a respectful distance, both Toby and the beast eyed each other with suspicion until Eduardo returned from the main house.

"Don't tell Mama." The boy said in Spanish and winked at Toby. From under his shirt he produced a banana which the greedy creature took from his hand and consumed in one sitting.

Toby enquired as to the name of the creature.

"Leona."

"No, no. Que es esto?" Toby asked.

"Esta iguana," the boy explained.

"Iguana," Toby repeated.

And for the remainder of the day, whenever Toby stepped outside, he would stop to study the strange lizard tethered to the cart.

Later that evening, after supper, Toby returned to his father's study. With the quill from the desk he wrote down the lines of the song he had remembered from his childhood days.

Three blinde mice,
Three blinde mice,
Dame Iulian,
Dame Iulian,
The Miller and his merry olde Wife,
Shee scrapte her tripe licke thou the knife

He opened the wooden box, took out the letter and below the rhyme copied down the code. Beneath the first group of symbols he entered his interpretation:

aI3 eIII3 aI2 a4, eIII3 fI6. bII3 b2 b3 cI4 f1 fI6
I S L E / S T. / C H R I S T

The first three words gave him great encouragement to continue and before too long much of the code had been deciphered.

ISLE/ST.CHRISTOPHER/TO/NEVIS/JAMESTOWN/CHURC
H/OF/ST.THOMAS/?B?E/

The symbols following the word *Thomas* had him perplexed for a while: they made no sense.

Toby stood by the window with a view across the valley.

On the road directly opposite the farm a man seemed to be looking towards the house; a skinny figure with a pale complexion. But that was all Toby could make of his appearance for, no sooner had he spotted him, the man was gone.

Toby returned to the message. That's when he remembered; when they used to play this game, there was always a folly to put off the 'spies and impostors'. Within an hour he had completed the message.

ISLE/ST.CHRISTOPHER/TO/NEVIS/JAMESTOWN/CHURCH/OF/ST.THOMAS/
?B?E/GRAVES/D.1668/MORTIMER/AND/KEACH.

That night, Toby lay in bed thinking about the message and what it all meant. Whenever they had played the game as children, the purpose was to uncover the clue which led to hidden presents around the house. But this code had been accompanied by a very poignant letter from a father to his loving family. And the location in the code was a good two hundred and fifty leagues from Jamaica. It would have to be a particularly important gift to make the journey to the Island of Nevis worthwhile. A legacy to the surviving children of Edward Hopkins, perhaps?

Hadn't that pirate Jack Bride on the *Lady Charlotte* mentioned that his father had taken part in the raids on Portobello. Did not he also make reference to bounty which mysteriously disappeared during those raids? What if his father has something to do with that! But what of Nevis? No-one had said anything about his father going there. Toby made a point to ask Magdalena about this in the morning.

That night Toby slept well: no dreams to interrupt his peace. Nor, during all the times he stayed at *La Bruma*, were there any other night disturbances.

In the light of day, the idea of a legacy from his father and his thought of hidden treasures seemed somewhat fanciful. However, Toby was keen to learn more about his father.

"Did he ever go away to other places?" he asked Magdalena.

"When he with me?"

"Yes."

"Portabello. He go the year before he died."

"What about before he met you, did he talk about voyages away? How about a place called Nevis?" Toby prompted. "Did he ever go there?"

Magdalena rested her hands on the counter and stared at the empty wall. It took a while before she answered. "Virginia, Barbados, Saint Christoph, Portobello, he talk 'bout them… Nevis? No, he not say 'bout Nevis."

She moved away towards the window.

"Do you not wish to talk about this?" Toby asked.

She turned around to face him and folded her arms. "It 'cos the two men who come here, they ask the same of me."

"What two men? What were they like?"

"Animals," Magdalena sucked through her teeth. "They say, they gonna kill my baby if I don't tell them."

"Tell them what?"

"Where Mister Edward keep his things. They say, he hide them. Lord, they was bad men, I tell you. They look everywhere, in the house, in the huts, everywhere. An' all the time the French one has my baby like he want to kill him. It only when some folks come to see the field that them go away." Magdalena searched the room "Where Edo?"

"He's just there, in the field."

This time Toby did feel guilty for burdening this on Magdalena. It was obviously disturbing for her. He stood alongside the woman, uncertain of what to do. "I'm sorry. I didn't mean to distress you."

Magdalena moved away. "You go call Edo. We go soon."

Chapter 17 – Spanish Town

It was mid-morning as they set off for Spanish Town and the sun was still bearable. So strange to take the route accompanied by Eduardo and his mother. The boy, dressed in a new shirt and a pair of breeches a few sizes too big, skipped ahead with frequent turns to check that he and Magdalena were still following. They passed the team of Surinamese Toby had seen the previous morning silently working the cane field.

"Would you consider hiring some of these men to help on the farm?" he asked.

Magdalena sucked and shook her head. "They is lazy an' will rob you when your back turned. No, I buy some good strong Negroes."

"How many would you need to get the farm working?"

"Five. I need five good strong men."

"I thought you said four yesterday?"

"Four workers and an overseer." Magdalena chuckled. "You is smart boy."

"An overseer?"

"To make men work hard an' not run to the hills."

"Do you have someone in mind?"

Magdalena didn't hesitate. "Carlos. He my cousin. Live in Santiago."

It was as if she had everything already planned.

"Do you think he will want to work at La Bruma?" asked Toby.

"Yeeess!" She sang the word. "Course he come! He say we look at men when next ship come in."

"You've already asked him?" Toby wondered how, considering her isolation and reluctance to invite visitors into the house, she managed to contact people so quickly.

"Aye, aye, aye!" she laughed. "How long you want wait to get this farm workin'?"

"Well," Toby shrugged. "As soon as possible, I suppose."

"It nearly November. We gotta get the land ready before next year or we miss another growin' season, right?"

Toby nodded.

"You want us sit in the sun all day like lazy lizards?" she added.

"No, of course not."

For the first time since his first visit to the farm, Toby was beginning to understand what his father saw in Magdalena.

Eduardo, having promised to show Toby the market in St Jago, was somewhat disappointed when they reached the Plaza and stood outside the Town Hall. Magdalena hesitated before they went inside.

"What troubles you?" asked Toby.

Magdalena looked up at the austere portico and heavy doors. "They is gonna ask me questions."

"So, I will be there to assist you."

Magdalena sucked through her teeth. "It not what you think."

"But I am accustomed to these people. I have dealings with them all the time."

Magdalena shook her head. "You is like a puppy. You think you know everything."

"There is something you have omitted to tell me?"

Again the woman made a sucking noise and shook her head. "There is things you maybe not wanna hear."

Toby shuffled his feet. He felt the anger rise. Arms folded, he turned to face her. "How can we work together and not be honest with each other?"

Eduardo, who had been silent for the past few minutes, was now tugging at his mother's sleeve. "Mama, cuando vamos a mercado?"

Magdalena ignored her son's request and stared at Toby who was pacing up and down the first three steps of the administrative building.

"Mama?" Edo insisted. "Mama!"

The woman, her eye fixed on Toby, bit her lower lip and yanked her arm away from her son's grasp.

"Fine!" she said. "We go."

Toby turned towards the woman expecting her to have given in to Eduardo's plea and to be heading for the market. Instead, Magdalena brushed past him and marched up the steps to the doors of the Town hall.

There were four chairs in the corridor outside the Registry of Land Grants. Eduardo chose to sit apart from his mother and Toby. He didn't say a word while they waited and remained silent when they were eventually called. Toby was prepared for a long and complicated process with many objections to his request. There was some difficulty in finding any record of Magdalena de Benitez being a free Negro. The clerk, a man of pallid complexion with an Italian accent, was called in to search the files. When he returned, he and the official exchanged a few words.

Once Toby assured them that he would be residing at La Bruma and that he intended employing Magdalena as Manager of the farm, the relevant documents were produced and the formalities of handing over the property to Toby were surprisingly straightforward. It transpired that there had been far too many absentee land owners in Jamaica and the council were keen to assign the farm over to him.

All the way from the civic plaza Magdalena linked her arm in Toby's while Eduardo skipped ahead and beckoned them to hurry.

The market was at its liveliest on a Friday. The ferry from Port Royal operated an extra service to account for the masses who poured into Spanish Town on that day. People of every class pushed and shoved with the promise of a good bargain or the hope of selling a few valuables to pay off a debt. At one point, while perusing the sale of some farming equipment, Toby and Magdalena lost sight of Edo. They searched through the crowd for a good five minutes before they found him at a stall which displayed a variety of trinkets and domestic items. In his hands was a bottle which he was holding up to the light.

Toby was about to go up to the boy when he noticed a man standing alongside him. Toby was sure he had seen the man somewhere before. He appeared to be haggling with the stall keeper over a pendant of the little Star of David and silver chain.

Edo spotted Toby and beckoned him over to show him his find. Toby studied the content of the bottle. Inside, crafted in the finest detail, was a model of a brigantine which looked remarkably similar to the *Chesapeake*. After a little bartering Toby purchased the item at a reasonable price. Eyes bright as stars, Edo ran over to his mother and showed her.

Toby looked around for the man who had been standing at the stall, but he had gone.

As soon as they arrived back at the farm Edo wanted to check the hog trap.

Everything was how they had left it. They discarded the meat which was attracting a lot of flies. Toby suggested they find what the pig was searching for and use that as bait. They dug around the spot near the tree where the hog had been burying its snout. Wrapped around the base of this tree was a vine and Edo pointed to a number of small tubers about the size of a potato attached to its branches. Some had fallen to the ground and it was probably these that the little hog was seeking out. They collected a dozen tubers and placed them in the centre of the lair, hoping that the following day might bring them better luck.

The next day Toby and Edo hurried up the track to investigate. There was no change; all was the same as the day before. As Toby was leaving La Bruma early on the following morning, he suggested that Edo just check the lair once each day so as not to frighten any prospective inquisitors.

The remainder of the day was spent fixing the cladding to the front of the house. In the absence of a long ladder, it was not possible to replace the roof tiles. Magdalena said she would find someone to fix them as soon as she had the funds.

Funds, or the lack of them, was a matter that had been on Toby's mind over the past few days. He asked Magdalena what she thought of Beatrice's friend, Elizabeth.

"Elizabeth!" she scowled. "That woman, she have the soul of the Devil!"

Toby wasn't expecting this reaction. "She has offered to contribute some finance towards the cost of our new vessel," he explained. "And I was considering accepting her offer."

She continued to shake her head. "Then you is mad, boy!"

"Well, it was just an idea." Toby thought it best to leave the subject alone. "I must return to Port Royal in the morning as I plan to sail two days hence. It may take a while before I can raise enough monies to pay for the house repairs, but I shall do what I can."

"I been here six year with no help, one more gonna make no difference," Magdalena shrugged. "Edo goin' to miss you. When you comin' back?"

"If all follows to plan, before the end of the year."

Chapter 18 – A Proposition

It was close to five when Toby arrived at the Spar and Halyard. Within one hour there was a knock on his door. One of the boys who tended the tables had been sent to tell him that a lady was awaiting his attention in the common room.

It was a general rule of the tavern that ladies were only permitted in private rooms at the advance payment of a surcharge; to which the management took every advantage. Toby was furious. This was the third time since he had taken lodging at the Spar and Halyard that his peace had been interrupted with this ruse, and each time he had to explain to the proprietor that he was not under any circumstances interested in entertaining a female in his room.

There were three customers as Toby stormed into the common room. The woman who was part of the ruse had her back to him with the pretence of looking through the window.

"I wish to make a complaint!" he demanded to the man at the counter. "This is the third time you have arranged a woman to call up to my room and on each occasion I . . ."

The woman by the window turned to face him. It was Elizabeth.

She gave him a coquettish smile. "Well, my dear Toby," she began. "As you have so many diversions, I promise not to entertain you for too long."

Toby could feel his cheeks flush. "Oh, I'm sorry. I didn't mean . . ."

The man at the counter was amused. "If you care to pay the surcharge, Sir, you can take the lady up to your –"

"No I would not!" Toby tried to control his temper. He turned to Elizabeth. "Would you care that we take a table outside?"

"That would be perfect."

They settled at one of the tables furthest from the entrance.

"There is a matter that concerns me." Elizabeth spoke with a sense of urgency.

Toby wasn't quite sure where the conversation was heading.

"What is it?" he said cautiously.

"Have you seen or know of the whereabouts of Beatrice since that night at the King's Rose?"

"No."

"Nor I. It is not in her character to be elusive so."

Toby was reminded of their first meeting. "No? I seem to recall, when we met at Leticia's, you had not seen her for –"

"Yes, yes. But that was for some other reason. This time is quite different."

From her expression, Toby could see that she was alarmed by her friend's absence.

"If I do see her, be assured I shall send word to you."

"Thank you." Elizabeth got up to leave.

"There is something I would ask of you," said Toby.

She sat back down. "Oh, yes. What might that be?" Her lighter mood was accompanied with a little flirtation.

Toby wasn't sure how to approach the subject. "When we had that chance meeting at the tobacco seller . . ." He hesitated.

"Go on, Toby."

"Well, I'm not sure if your offer was intended as a serious –"

"My dear Toby, do you wish to . . . how shall I express it? Do you care to dance with me again?"

For the second time Toby felt the colour rise to his cheeks. "No, no. I do not mean that. Well, of course, that would be . . . " Toby regained his composure. "What I refer to is your offer of financial assistance."

Elizabeth sat up. "Oh, I see. This is for your trading venture, is it not?"

"That is so."

She leaned forward and placed her hands under her chin. "I am curious to know more of your plans."

"Myself and John Fowler, the Mate of the Chesapeake Venture, that's the vessel we had the misfortune to lose at Maracaibo."

"Yes, I do remember you telling me, Toby."

"Well, Mister Fowler and myself are in the process of purchasing another vessel, modest in comparison to our previous brig, and we plan to extend our trading links to include the southern colonies."

"And am I to presume this would include Jamaica?"

"It would, yes." Toby wondered how John would take to this commitment.

"Where else do you plan to trade?" she asked.

"I have already good connections in the colonies of Virginia, Maryland and the Plymouth colony and we hope to secure new ones in Barbados and Saint Lucia."

"You make no mention of New Amsterdam?"

"New York?"

"New Amsterdam, New York, whatever they will next name it. Do you plan to trade there?"

"If it should be worth our while, yes."

"And how much finance are you seeking?"

Toby was caught on the spot. This woman was so perceptive in business. Should he err on the side of frugality or exaggerate the request?

"Five hundred escudos," he ventured.

This didn't appear to deter Elizabeth and, after a few more searching questions regarding finances, they arranged to meet the following day.

"Shall we say at four tomorrow?" she suggested.

"Fine. With myself and John Fowler?"

"Of course."

"Where shall we meet?"

Elizabeth looked out across at the vessels moored in the bay. "This place would be appropriate."

Toby watched this woman, a beauty by most accounts, walk away in the direction of the cut which led to New Street. He was about to return to his lodging when a man in militia uniform approached his table.

"Good day, Sir. Would you be Mister Hopkins?"

"I am," Toby replied cautiously.

Without invitation, the man squeezed his portly frame between the table and bench and sat down. "The office at Fort Charles inform me that you have been making enquiries about your father, Captain Edward Hopkins."

"I am, although I was. I have now located him, thank you."

The Sergeant paused for a moment and studied Toby. "My name is Smithson, Sergeant Thomas Smithson. I am investigating the case of William Cooper of St. Andrews."

The man was about forty years of age. His moustache and side whiskers reminded Toby of a species of wild bear he had occasion to see in the upper reaches of the Hudson River.

"Cooper?" Toby frowned. "I am sorry Sergeant. The only Cooper I am familiar with is Michael Cooper, who lives in the Colony of Maryland."

"No, sir. This is Lieutenant William Cooper of Villa Madre in the parish of St. Andrews, here in Jamaica." Toby wondered if this man had taken a wrong tack.

"You haven't heard of the St. Andrews October Murders?"

"Forgive me, Sergeant, I am new to this town."

The man took in a deep breath. "It happened four years ago" He exhaled slowly through his nose which emitted a soft wheezing sound. "In October 1671. William Cooper was commissioned here from Barbados that same year. Both he and his wife had moved to their residence at . . . " The man glanced down at his notebook, "La Principe de la Madre."

Toby smiled, amused by the sergeant's attempt at Spanish.

"It was there," Smithson continued, "at their home, that the unfortunate event took place." He looked up and eyed Toby closely, "T'were late in the evening when the bodies were discovered, in a storehouse behind the Coopers' residence."

Toby traced his thumbnail along the edge of the table. One unfortunate consequence of sitting alone at a table in a public place is that it encourages the most bizarre individuals to impose on you.

"Both the Lieutenant and his wife," continued Smithson, "were tied to the standing posts of the building. Cooper was shot in the head and his poor wife had been stripped of her clothing and tortured to death." The Sergeant bit his lower lip. As he did so, his moustache twisted to form a grimace. "The floor was covered in blood. The poor girl was as white as a Plymouth shift. All down the sides of her body was flayed with a knife, or similar instrument. T'was like a cook would prepare a herring for the stove. It is my suspicion that her husband had been forced to observe the whole ordeal." The sergeant paused for a moment. "And what made it worse, the young woman was heavy with child."

This was obviously not a first-hand account, thought Toby. He rubbed the scab along his right arm. "Forgive me, Sergeant, but what has this to do with my father?"

Smithson cleared his throat. "When they inspected the house they found some letters which had been addressed to Cooper in Barbados two years before. The house was a mess, I tell you. All the Cooper's artefacts had been thrown across the floor in every room, without the least respect for the owners. The letters had been left on a table in the study, open for all to see."

As the couple were about to be killed, Toby doubted the state of their rooms would really have concerned the victims. He was beginning to wonder if this man was an impostor. There were so many strange people in this town, and plenty of places where one could purchase a military uniform: the Merchant's Inn for one. "I still do not see what this has to do with me."

"One of these letters was sent by Captain Hopkins and referred to a voyage, which it seems both he and Lieutenant Cooper had made, to the Spanish Colonies. It also referred to a prize taken on this voyage."

Toby straightened up. "What prize?"

The Sergeant shifted his position. "That is all the letter stated, Sir. It did not give any further detail." He looked down at his notebook and cleared his throat again. "Perhaps you can tell me. Do you recall your father ever referring to a visit by anyone connected with Lieutenant Cooper?"

"This is the first I have heard that name. As I said before, the only Cooper I know lives in –"

"Yes, thank you Sir. I have noted this." The sergeant ran his fingers through his whiskers. "One other thing. Does the name Keach mean anything to you?"

"Not that I recall," Toby lied.

The man studied Toby for a moment. It seemed he was about to enquire something further, but changed his mind. Instead, he tucked the notebook away in his jacket and stood up. "Thank you for your help, Mister Hopkins. Should anything come to your thoughts concerning this matter, you can find me at the Militia Office at Fort Charles." The sergeant studied Toby again. "You know where that is?"

"Yes I do. As you know, I have already been there." Toby recalled his visit to Fort Charles and how unhelpful the desk sergeant had been there.

"Oh yes, of course. Well, thank you again Mister Hopkins."

Toby wondered if the militia believed there was more than one person involved in this crime.

"Could I ask, Sergeant, have you arrested the murderers?"

"No, Sir, they are still free. The case has been re-opened due to recent events."

"Recent events?"

"I am not at liberty to say more than that, Sir."

Toby thought this typical of militia personnel. It gave them an air of mystery in an otherwise unimaginative profession. The *recent events* were probably a fanciful muse devised to bring new light to an otherwise unsolvable case.

"Would it be possible to see the letter my father sent to this man?" Toby asked.

"I am not at liberty to grant that either, Sir. The letter has been retained at the office as possible evidence pertaining to the crime."

Toby watched the Sergeant wheeze his heavy frame towards the door. After two steps, he turned back. "One more thing, Mister Hopkins."

"Yes, Sergeant?"

"Have you had any news of your father?"

Toby hesitated before replying. "Yes. My father passed on six years ago. On a mission from the Militia here in Jamaica." Toby paused. "But I thought you would know this."

Smithson just nodded and ran his fingers through his whiskers. "I wonder. Can you tell me where you were between the hours of midnight and five in the morning of the first of this month?"

"The first?"

"Yes, Sir. That would be a Tuesday, just short of two weeks ago."

Toby though for a moment. "I was lodging at the King's Rose off Lime Street."

The sergeant raised his brow. "The King's Rose, you say? Can anyone confirm that, Sir?"

Toby was puzzled by this enquiry. He thought the man seemed tired, probably overworked.

"I should think the proprietor will account for me."

Smithson frowned as he attempted to scribble with what was left of his stub of a pencil. "And did you happen to meet a man by the name of Rubens there?"

"Rubens? No, I don't know anyone of that name."

"I see. Well, that'll be all for now." The sergeant looked Toby in the eye as he tucked away his notebook. "Oh, you're not planning on leaving Port Royal for a while, are you Sir?"

"Not for a while, no Sergeant," Toby lied.

He watched the man move through the door which led into the tavern.

It was clear the letter hadn't given away much. However, the reference to *the prize* in connection to voyages to the Spanish Colonies must be the reason the militia were so interested in this crime. There was also mention of the name Keach. The Sergeant didn't give away his own thoughts to that name. Maybe he believed Keach was one of the murderers.

If his father was involved in the disappearance of the treasure, why didn't he tell Magdalena about it? Surely, if he loved her, he would want to share the spoils with her. On the other hand, it was good fortune that she didn't know. Only one year after Eduardo was born, the very same year the Cooper murder took place, Magdalena had a visit from two men who she described as animals. Lucky for her and Eduardo they were interrupted by someone, or else neither of them would be here now.

Toby traced his finger along the line of his chin. Someone, either Cooper or his wife, must have let the secret out soon after they arrived in Jamaica. If Cooper had known about Toby's father's death two years earlier, why hadn't he kept the treasure for himself? What if this *is* what he did? Toby had the dreadful thought; the expedition to Nevis he planned to undertake could be a complete waste of time. It could turn out that this man, Lieutenant Cooper, may have already been there to collect the booty and hidden it somewhere else. Or worse still' it had been discovered by his murderers. But, if that was true, why would these villains come up to search Magdalena's house straight after dealing with Cooper?

If only Toby had more time. If they weren't sailing in two days, he and John could go up to Cooper's house to have a look for themselves.

Considering what the sergeant had told him, it could be that Eduardo and his mother would be at risk while he's away. Toby made a vow to pay a return visit to the Militia Office at Fort Charles before they set sail.

Chapter 19 – Ogres and Beasts

The sun was low as Edo and his mother headed back down the beaten track toward the house. Magdalena, her heavy breasts juggling beneath the sweat-soaked dress, paced herself down the last few steps of the path. Following a few feet behind, Eduardo kept a firm grip of the loaded cart which was now ploughing its way between the rocks at the base of the hill. He wished Mister Toby hadn't left so soon. He said he would be back in a few months, but how long is that? Now everything was back to the way it was before he came.

It was when they reached the flat at the bottom of the field, the boy had a feeling something was not quite right. He rested the cart down and looked around. Nothing out of place, all seemed to be as it should be.

His mother turned and gave him a look. The boy picked up the cart and followed her to the door of the field-house. She was about to step inside.

"Espera, Mama! Wait!"

Magdalena frowned. "C'est quoi?"

Eduardo shrugged. "Don't know."

His mother shook her head and muttered something as she disappeared into the shadows.

Eduardo waited outside.

It was over a minute before Magdalena returned. She came up and pressed her son's head into her soft belly. "Silly boy. Sometimes I think you is crazy." She gave one more neck-wrenching squeeze before she released him. "Now, you unload the cart," she said. "I go make us a nice cup of molasses water."

Eduardo pushed the cart inside the dark building and rested it down beside the table. He crept around the room without a sound. First, over to the stone trough; he peeked over the edge – nothing – just Leona asleep on his rock. The iguana lifted its head, opened one eye and surveyed the boy. Eduardo pressed a finger to his lips. The lizard let out an indignant sigh and settled back down to sleep.

Next the witches' cooking pots. Eduardo crouched to check between the stills before venturing to the end of the row. He peeked around; nothing there either. He looked up at the largest vat; even a monster wouldn't be able get in there because the top was sealed. A *duppy* could, but Mama says they don't like dark places and you only find them among the mangroves. The only other place was the chest which had all the tools he was not allowed to touch. It had been locked for over three weeks now. So, all was safe: no monsters here. Eduardo returned to the cart.

He lifted out the first two pods and held them poised over the table. His drink would be getting cold by now. He placed them back in the cart and headed out into the sunshine.

At the kitchen door something made him stop. He moved the wooden box to the window and stepped up.

His mother was sitting at the table with her arms resting behind the back of the chair. It was so strange, for the moment he saw her, she caught sight of him too. Eduardo stepped down.

As soon as he opened the door, his mother called in a low voice. "Edo, run! Hide!" she urged. "Go! Now, Edo! Go get help." Her face showed she meant it.

A figure appeared in the hallway behind; a man. A man with the eyes of a snake. As soon as he saw Eduardo, he called out down the hall.

"Mitchell!"

The boy didn't wait to hear the rest. He shot across the level and headed straight for the wood which ran up the hill. Once he reached the shaded trees, he found the path and made his way up through the tangled thicket. He didn't stop once, not until he reached the top. Not even to take a breath.

Thank God the hog trap was still unbroken. The boy moved the branches at the edge aside and slipped into the pit three feet below. Hardly daring to breathe, he sat very still.

The minutes dragged with aching slowness. An age before the first crack of a dry branch could be heard. The sound came from the top of the hill where the head of the field meets the copse. The footsteps were pressing further into the wood now. Without a machete the task would be near impossible, but the person was determined. Branches cracked as the grunting figure forced his way through the dense undergrowth, right up towards the clearing where the hog trap lay.

The boy's heart pounded in his ears as the sound got closer. He bit down hard on his lip as the monster broke through the final thicket that bordered into the clearing. He squeezed his eyes shut.

Many minutes went by without a single sound from the world above: a silence filled with threat. It took great courage before Eduardo could persuade himself to open an eye. He looked up to the roof of his lair. A shadow had formed across the thin covering of branches and leaves. The boy screwed his eyes and tried to focus on the place where he had first entered the pit. He swallowed hard. Towering from the edge of his hide, were the legs of a giant. And hanging from the ogre's belt, was a heavy wooden cudgel. Eduardo took a deep breath and closed his eyes.

He waited in the silent pit, waited and waited. It wasn't till he heard the whistle of a cowbird in the branches above that Eduardo dared to open his eyes again. The shadow was gone. The evening sunlight filtered through the leaves above his head. There was no figure. Could he have imagined it? Mama was always telling him not to make up stories. Maybe it was true, he did imagine things. Could it be that he had dreamed up the whole thing? There was no monster chasing him after all. What an idiot: *Estupido*!

The boy stood up and pushed his head through the opening. He took a breath of fresh air and rested his elbows at the edge ready to heave himself out. Just as he straightened up he was gripped by the upper arms and lifted high off the ground. The monster! And it had wings! Eduardo kicked and wriggled to get away, but the bird's talons kept their grip. It's going to take me over the field and out across the bay to far off lands! Eduardo gave one almighty kick and struck the bird's leg.

"Ouch! You slippery little bastard!" the bird spat. "Hold still, or I'll beat your brains to a mush, you hear?"

The monster had now changed to a man. It tucked the boy under its arm. All the way down the hill they went; crashing though the bushes, dodging the trees along the path and out into the sun near the sheds. All the way until they reached the kitchen door the boy squirmed and wriggled under the monster's arm.

"Got him, Mister G," said the bird monster.

Snake eyes was standing over the chair where Mama sat. And behind her was another; a man who looked just like the bear-fighter in the market in Santiago last year. This one had a knife. The man fixed his snake eyes on Edo then spoke to the monster. "In the stone house outside there is a long trench. Tie the boy and put him in there. But before you finish, be making sure you cover him up good. You understand?"

"Yes, Mister G. He'll be good an' buried when I finished with 'im."

"Listen," the snake hissed. "Don't you go doing any more than I say. Just tie him and bury him. I am making myself clear?"

"Yes, Mister G."

The monster tightened his grip on Edo and pulled him to the big shed. He held his wrists together in one claw and wrapped a line of jute rope round and round his arms until it got to the end. He picked up the boy and dropped him into the trough. There was a scraping sound, then a thump as a pile of sand landed over the boy's legs. The sand was heavy. Edo tried to turn but he couldn't move. He watched the metal cover slide over the trench. All went dark. Then came a crash, then another. Like a canon from the harbour, the roof of his tunnel exploded as each of Mama's Cassava weights landed on the the cover. Now there would be no escape! The boy tried to turn. He tried and tried but couldn't move. The minutes went by, an hour, maybe even more. The air was thick, damp in his chest, too hard to suck in. Edo closed his eyes. The dark was heavy, like that night they got home late from the festival last month. All Edo wanted to do was sleep. The darkness closed in.

It was his coughing that woke him: he was almost choking. He tried to sit up but there was no feeling in his body. He lay still in the dark and tried to stay calm. A spray of sand hit his face, then another.

"Leona!" With all this going on, he had completely forgotten about him.

The iguana, who had been disgruntled that its home had been rearranged, was occupied with clearing the sand from the exit to the trench. Spray after spray of damp grit was thrown behind the creature as it headed for the outside world. The boy felt the first wave of warm air brush against his cheek. He took a deep breath. A few more minutes and he could move his feet.

As soon as he crawled out into the warm glow of the evening sun, Edo untied the creature and placed it on the ground near the door. "You go run and hide," he said. "Go, before the monster comes back."

He looked over to the house: the way was clear. He kept low and crept towards the building, turned off down the overgrown path squashed between the main house and the outbuilding. Once on the road, he headed for St Jago. He ran and ran as fast as his legs would take him. Bea would be there: at the house in Santiago. That's what Mama said. She made him promise not go there. Told him not to say anything to anyone about Bea. But this was different: there were monsters at the farm.

It was almost dark when he got to the town. Two more streets and he would be there. What if Bea wasn't there? If the house was empty, what should he do then? He arrived at the little white-washed building in Calle Majon and banged on the door. It stayed closed. He banged again, as hard as his fist could stand.

"Aye, aye, aye. Qué te pasa? Quién es?" the voice was Aunt Juana.

Edo bent forward to catch his breath. "Es Eduardo," he panted. The door swung open and Juana's frame filled the entrance. "Edo! Qué te pasa?"

Chapter 20 – **Intruder**

On the Tuesday morning, Toby and John found the Dunstan moored alongside a jetty at the east end of the harbour. She rode so high in the water that it was impossible to secure a gangplank on such a narrow jetty: the only way to board was by a ladder which had already been set fast amidships. At least it gave them the opportunity to inspect the work done to the hull of the vessel. The shipwright had given them one day to check the inventory and inspect the repairs before they were required to pay the balance. Toby read out each item on the list while his Mate checked the condition.

Everything appeared to be in good order. However, as the vessel had been transported from the beach on two jibs and the mizzen, the remaining sails had been stowed away in a locker below the forecastle deck. It took the two men most of the morning to drag the canvasses out from the confined space. They stretched each sail across the main hatch cover to check for wear and tear. There was no shade out on the deck and, as the day grew hotter, tempers shortened.

"So, the fore-topsail is fine." Toby ticked the item on his list. A bead of sweat dropped from the tip of his nose and landed neatly onto the centre of the page.

"Fore course sail, I think you'll find Captain."

Toby sighed. "No, we've already checked that." He marched over to the stack of canvasses piled neatly against the poop bulkhead. He lifted the top two and prodded the third one with his index finger. "It's this one, here!" He gave his Mate an exasperated look.

"That's the main topsail, Sir. This one," John lifted the corner of the canvas spread out across the hatch, "is the fore course."

"So, correct me if I'm wrong. What you are suggesting is that we rig that sail up along the first spar of the foremast and stretch it out to the end of the yard – even if it rips?"

"T'wont rip, Sir."

That did it! Toby stomped over to the locker room and returned with a coil of rope. He gave one end to John to hold at one corner of the canvas while he knotted his kerchief around the rope where the sail ended.

Without a word, Toby coiled up the rope, slung it over his shoulder and scrambled up the ratlines to the masthead. He eased his way along the yard and attached his line to the end of the spar.

John sat at the edge of the hatch, crossed his legs and took out his pipe. Giving the occasional glance to his captain, he filled the bowl. Toby, shirt soaked in sweat, was now edging his way along the main spar thirty feet above his head.

While the town of Port Royal was hiding from the uncompromising heat of the midday sun, to the casual onlooker, a man could be seen balancing at the very end of a yard arm forty feet above the clear blue waters of the bay. Below him, on the hatch cover of the main hold, sat another man sucking on his hand-carved pipe. A cloud of blue smoke drifted across the quiet waters of the bay as the man aloft made his way along the spar. He was halfway across the starboard arm when he seemed to change his mind. The man on deck glanced up to note that several coils remained over his captain's shoulder; a good measure before the loop marked with a red kerchief. He sucked at his pipe and followed the flight of a solitary pelican gliding across the still waters of the harbour.

At about eleven before noon they were surprised to see Midshipman Matthew Wilkins, step over the rail. The boy said he'd been staying with a friend in temporary lodgings the previous night and they had to vacate the room by ten that morning. News had got around that his Captain and Mate were inspecting a new vessel.

"Is this it?" As soon as his feet hit the deck, Matthew took a quick glance forward and aft and frowned. "Not very big, is it."

Before Toby could answer, John intervened. "That's as maybe, lad. But 'tis the only ship up for sail right now."

"But I thought you said we were going back home." Matthew still looked puzzled. "Not just trading around the coast here."

Toby was about to explain when John continued. "What would you prefer, lad? Continue lodging in this town with your temporary friends until we find a larger vessel, or head back home as soon as possible?"

Matthew looked back over his shoulder towards the town and appeared to be considering these options. It hadn't gone unnoticed the kind of company Matthew had been keeping since they arrived in Port Royal, and, considering his age, this was of some concern to the Mate.

"I think, while you're here, you can lend a hand and help us with this inventory. What do you think, Captain?"

Toby, who was looking up at the mast he had descended, still puzzled about the length of the spar, glanced back at Midshipman Wilkins and the Mate. "Er, what was that again, Mister Fowler?"

"I was saying to young Matthew here, he could help us with this muster. I'm sure he could do with the extra wage."

"Yes, quite so, Mister Fowler." He turned to Matthew. "Go down to the fo'c's'le locker and you'll see some hawsers coiled on deck. Fetch them up here and lay them alongside the pile of canvasses over there."

"One at a time, mind," John added. "No point in damaging yerself."

As Toby and the Mate continued to work their way through the pile of sailcloth, Matthew occasionally appeared with a coil of rope slung over his shoulder. After a while the stack of rope alongside the diminishing pile of sails gradually got higher.

It was as they were inspecting a topsail, a scream was heard from the forecastle deck. Both men dropped the canvas and ran forward.

When they reached Matthew he was lying on deck with his hands clawing at the rope which had somehow wrapped itself around his neck. It took both men, with much effort, a good minute to unravel the coils from the boy's throat.

Once the boy had got back his breath, he appeared to have recovered and both John and Toby thought he must have been acting out a game to fool them. However, on close inspection of Matthew's neck, the rope had left an impression; marks about his throat, like the scalding of a hot wire. And it was the same with his hands; a blistering across his palms where he had attempted to release the coils. And yet, when Toby and John inspected their own hands, there was nothing.

Although Matthew said he no longer felt any pain, both men suggested he should find the purser, Mr Davies, and get it seen to.

After the boy had gone the two men both came to the same conclusion: that this was yet another example of of Matthew's afflictions. But what to do about it, they had no idea, apart from pray the manifestations would eventually go away.

It was one hour after noon. While Toby and John were still sorting through the heap of canvases on the main deck of the Dunstan, a skinny man stood outside the door of their room at the Spar and Halyard. He gave the door a quiet tap and waited. From the bunch of irons in his hand he selected the first and tried the lock. The key failed to turn. He chose another. This time he had it. The iron turned with a clunk. The man slipped inside and took his bearings: with no window to let in the daylight, the room was dark. In the gloom the man could just make out the shape of an oil lamp at the table with some flints conveniently placed beside it. He measured the distance and closed the door.

Once the room was illuminated, he set about his task. First the items on the table. From the pocket of his jerkin he took a scrap of paper and studied all the words inscribed on it.

Edward Hopkins, Cptn. E. Hopkins, Edward James, father, Father

He picked up the first item; a hand written letter which started with the words; *My Dearest Toby* and ended with *Your loyal and dearest friend, Elizabeth Thomas*. None of these words appeared to match those he had been given. The next looked promising; another letter which, this time, began *My dearest Sarah*, but this also proved to be a false lead.

The only other items on the table were a ship's log and a cloth-bound book. He picked up the book and flicked through the pages; nothing hidden between them. He placed it carefully back on the table, adjusting its position a fraction.

There were two beds in the room. Thrown across the first were a number of vestments and a seaman's kitbag. He eased it open and reached inside. The bag was stuffed with clothes and the only things he could find were a collection of modelling tools, two clay pipes and a volume of navigation tables. The man stood back and studied the room thoughtfully.

There was a knock at the door. The man held his ground; he was not prepared for this.

Another knock.

He took his cudgel from his belt and moved to the door. He opened it a fraction. The figure through the gap appeared to be little more than a boy; a creole of about fifteen years.

"What do you want? I'm very busy!" said the skinny man.

"You is Captain Hopkins?" The boy was out of breath.

"Yes."

"I got important message. It from Miss Beatrice."

"Go on."

"She say you is in danger. Three men come to farm. Three bad men. They hurt Miss Magdalena. . ." The boy caught his breath, "but she all right now."

"Good. What else did she say?"

"Miss Beatrice say you must get away. The men come look for you. She say one is. . .is a. . . duh," the boy stamped his foot three times on the floor.

"A Dutchman?" the intruder suggested.

"Yes, yes. That what she say. She say you must hide. Go from here." The boy thought for a moment. "That the message."

The door closed as the boy had finished the final word.

The man looked about the room. There was another kitbag, under the second bed. He pulled it out. Apart from a few items of clothing, the bag contained the Holy Book, a collection of papers bound with string with the title; *An Essay to Revive the Antient Education of Gentlewomen, in Religion, Manners, Arts and Tongues,* and a small box. The collection of papers didn't promise much. He opened the box. Apart from the ring, there were a number of worthless items, a paper with some jottings and a letter. He studied the jottings.

ISLE/ST.CHRISTOPHER/TO/NEVIS/JAMESTOWN/CHURCH/OF/ST.THOMAS/EM?E/GRAVES/D.1668/MORTIMER/AND/KEACH.

These were in a script he was not familiar with and didn't seem to follow the usual way of writing. Also, none of the writing appeared to resemble the words he was asked to look for. He turned his attention to the letter and screwed his eyes at the bottom of the page. There were some more strange jottings, similar to the ones on the paper. However, just above this was a more familiar script: *Your ever loving husband and father, Edward James Hopkins.*

The man pulled the scrap of paper from his pocket. He looked from one to the other. There were four words at the end of the group; *father, Edward, James and Hopkins*. They all seemed to match.

The man pocketed the letter and replaced the remaining items in the kitbag. He took a good look around the room before extinguishing the lamp. He then left, taking care to lock the door behind him.

Chapter 21 – **A New Partner**

For the remainder of the afternoon, Toby and the Mate checked the inventory of the little Dutch Fluyt in silence. It was not until they were sitting on the bench outside the *Spar and Halyard* that Toby brought up the subject of his father's letter.

"Nevis, you say?" John sat with his back against the wall. "I doubt they'd agree to that."

"We don't tell them," Toby said.

The Mate gave Toby a sideways look. "They may look stupid to you, Captain, but methinks a few of 'em can tell the difference 'twix Nevis and Virginia!"

"No, I mean we only tell the crew of our change of course after we cast off from here. It is of the utmost importance that no-one in this town knows of our plan." Toby paused. "Anyway, Nevis is not too far off course. And we would need to take on fresh water before we reach Virginia."

"Hmm…" John's main concern seemed to be the immediate problem of the *Dunstan's* draught. "I reckon we should load her up with logwood. She'll not fare too well in rough weather such as she is."

"If it turns out to be true, I'll not be able to administer this alone," Toby said. "Would you consider coming in with me?"

"That's what we agreed, Captain. But there'll be no need to sail to the Campechy coast. There's a sloop just come in from there loaded up with logwood. I can set up a deal with the master if you wish."

"No. I mean, yes, that's fine. But I was talking about the letter from my father."

"Oh, that. Well if you think so, Captain."

"So we'll go ahead with it, as planned?"

"Load up with Logwood?" John was confused.

"Set a course for Nevis," Toby said.

"Logwood or Nevis? You lost me there, Captain."

"Both then. How much can you put in for the cargo?"

"I just assigned most of my bounty to my share of the vessel." John counted quietly to himself. "Thirty-six gold cobs and twenty-three escudo pieces. That'll be all I've got left over."

"So how about three to ten?" said Toby

"For the logwood, or to help you with your bounty?"

"Both."

"Done. I'll sort the logwood with the mate of the sloop when we're finished here." John stretched his arms behind his head. "I said I'd meet some of the crew in town later."

Toby was about to discourage him, but he let it pass. They had been docked in this town for two weeks now and, despite the many temptations on offer, John had abstained from heavy drinking and proved that he had the problem under control. He was as keen as his captain to sail out of the place, so what harm could there be if he met up with the crew for a farewell celebration on their last night?

However, there was very little time to organise the cargo and Toby hoped these diversions wouldn't hold them up. He nodded over to the Dunstan. "You think it possible to load up from that narrow jetty, John?"

"It'll have to be from a lighter. Out of sight from the customs house, if you know what I mean, Sir." John gave him a knowing look.

"I meant for the general cargo, not the logwood."

John glanced over to the jetty. "That'll be fine there. But, for the logwood, would be best if we moor out in the bay."

"Well, so be it. But let me know the arrangements before tonight, please."

"Isn't that her?" The Mate was looking over Toby's shoulder.

Two figures were walking from the direction of Queen Street; a lady in a fashionable dress accompanied by an older man with the attire of a bank merchant. The two looked somewhat out of place as they approached quayside tavern.

Toby and John stood up to greet them.

"Good afternoon, Elizabeth, I hope the day treats you well. This is Mister Fowler, Mate of the Dunstan and partner of our business venture."

Elizabeth extended her arm.

"A delight to make your acquaintance, my Lady." John took her hand and kissed her fingers with surprising eloquence.

"And I also." Elizabeth seemed as impressed as Toby. "And this is Joseph Brown, my advisor in matters of finance."

Toby shook the man's hand. He nodded at the empty bench across the table from where they had been sitting. "I hope this is an appropriate location for our meeting?"

"Here is fine, Toby," said Elizabeth.

After the introductions and ordering of beverages, the four settled down to business.

"If I was to give one thousand escudos," Elizabeth got straight to the point, "I would require a share of thirty percent of the business profit." She looked from one to the other.

"Thirty percent?" Toby frowned. "But that is a large share, and we only need funds to the value of five hundred escudos."

"On the contrary, five hundred escudos would soon be taken up with consignment purchases and taxes. You will be left with nothing to expand your business." She turned to her advisor. "Is that not true, Mister Brown?"

"It certainly is, Mistress Thomas." The man beside her went though many points concerning this business proposition which he and Elizabeth had previously discussed. And it was soon apparent that both Toby and John, in their haste to set sail, had not considered many financial aspects of their venture.

"So, if we did accept your generous offer, Mistress Thomas." John was in his element. ""What advantage would there be in taking you on as a partner?"

"For one, you would also be taking on a very astute financial advisor in Mister Brown."

Her companion nodded in appreciation. "And secondly," Elizabeth continued, "I have some very good connections."

"And, if I may ask, do your connections extend beyond the bounds of Jamaica?" Toby asked.

"Yes, they do."

"I see." Toby rubbed his chin. "Would you mind if I discuss this with John for a moment?"

John stood up. "I'll ask that the serving wench refresh your glasses while the Captain and me take a stroll."

"That is very gracious of you, Mister Fowler."

The smile which Elizabeth gave John reminded Toby of that first meeting in an alley not too far from where they were seated now.

The two partners of the Dunstan paced the quayside.

"But how do you know she's telling the truth, John?"

"Of course she has connections. It's her business."

"Whoring?"

"Yes whoring. She's clearly very successful at it. I would guess she's amongst the most well connected persons in this island. We should take her on, Captain."

"She's seducing you. Do you not see that?"

John stopped in his tracks. "So that's it. You don't take a liking to the idea that I might get along with someone who you prefer to distance yourself from?"

"No. That's not it, Mister Fowler. The fact is, I am concerned as to the reason why she is so keen to join us."

"Maybe she just sees it as a good proposition." John ran his fingers through his whiskers. "With respect, Captain. I think you should have a little more confidence in your judgements."

"Ha! And look where that's got . . . " Toby cleared his throat. "Look, we've kept them waiting long enough. What's our decision?"

"I say take her on," said John.

"I say, let's ask about these connections first. If they are believable, then I will agree."

"Fair enough, Captain."

John and Toby returned to the table.

"Well, before we give our decision," said Toby, "Can you give an example of one of your connections which would be to our advantage?"

Elizabeth studied the two gentlemen across the table. She leaned forward "You must promise me not to repeat what I am about to say."

"Agreed," said John. He gave his captain a nudge.

"Agreed."

Elizabeth waited until a customer passed through into the tavern. She sat up straight. "There is rumour that in Virginia, where I understand you gentlemen are bound, there are plans to increase the levy on tobacco. This being so, a number of planters are in a hurry to sell their existing stock at a very reasonable price."

"But surely, any ship trading with that colony would be able to take advantage of the situation," said Toby.

"Not quite so simple. The English have set up a new office. I cannot recall the name." She looked towards her advisor.

"Lords of Trade," said Mr Brown. "The reason for the levy is to avoid a sharp decline in the price of tobacco, they have now set a fixed price on all exports – "

"Yes, well," Elizabeth continued, "the only way some of these planters can survive is to bypass these duties and conduct their trade in secrecy, with trusted associates." Elizabeth took a sip from her glass. "The man responsible for organising this clandestine trade is a good acquaintance of mine. So, if you should wish to 'take me on'," she smiled at John. "I can arrange an introduction which could be very profitable for our venture."

John and the captain looked at each other.

Elizabeth turned to Toby. "I would also suggest that I ask an acquaintance of mine, who has expertise in plant management, to take a look at that farm you have recently acquired. With a view to running it more efficiently."

"How did you know about that?" Toby was perplexed. "I only signed the papers on Friday."

Elizabeth smiled. "These things have a way of reaching me."

All were quiet for a few moments at the table outside the Spar and Lanyard.

Elizabeth was the first to break the silence. "Well gentlemen. Have you come to a decision?"

Toby nodded to his Mate.

"Yes we have, Mistress Thomas," said John. "We would be more than happy to take you on board on your terms."

Elizabeth laughed. "Then, I too am more than happy to join you."

They all raised their glasses to the success of their new partnership.

"What of this profitable introduction?" asked Toby.

"Well, I suggest that you continue with your journey to Virginia." Elizabeth said. "How long will it take you to reach James Town?"

Toby looked at his Mate.

"I'd say the fluyt will make a headway of no more than six to eight knots." John scratched his beard. "So, by my reckoning, I'd say at least six days."

"Don't forget we plan to avoid the *Windward Passage*," reminded Toby.

"Oh yes, the detour." He looked across to his captain and raised an eyebrow. "Of course that'll add another week to our journey."

Toby declined to comment.

"So, gentlemen, that should give me enough time to contact my man in James Town," continued Elizabeth. "I will also forward a letter of introduction and more detail of the assignment for you to pick up when you dock in Virginia."

"Seems simple enough," said Toby.

"If all goes according to our design, I suggest you take this cargo to the New Delft Trading Company in Krommeval Street, New Amsterdam."

"Now called New York," said Mr Brown.

"Yes, yes, New York. They will give anything for a consignment of quality tobacco."

"But surely there are restrictions on trading there? The very reason I have not visited this town thus far."

"As you are probably aware, Captain Hopkins," Mr Brown placed his hands on the table. "There have recently been some modifications to the Navigation Act which has further restricted the trading of foreign ships in the English colonies – particularly with the Dutch. In some ports foreign vessels are forbidden entry altogether." He looked at the two men seated opposite him. "The fact that your vessel, Gentlemen, is of Dutch design, may be to your advantage when entering the port of New York. And, as it is registered in an English colony and manned by an English crew, you will have the further advantage in being permitted to enter the port of James Town and free to conduct your business there."

"But surely this new law will not permit me to trade tobacco with the Delft Company in New York?" said Toby.

"Providing your consignment remains undetected in Virginia," said Elizabeth. "This would be a simple matter to arrange . . . should you have the right connections, of course. However, I would say it would be wise to keep the details of our business scheme between ourselves. There is enough political unrest in that colony that any unconventional dealings might be viewed suspiciously."

Toby shifted in his seat and glanced towards his Mate.

"And, I'm sure," continued Elizabeth, "there is nothing to be concerned about. Everything will work to our financial advantage. When you reach New Amster – New York, ask for Pieter van Kool. Give him my greetings and tell him 'the kitten is asleep'. He will understand. He will give you a very good price for your cargo."

Mr Brown took a watch from his pocket. He leaned across to Elizabeth. "It's almost a quarter before the hour."

"Oh, yes. Thank you Joseph." Elizabeth rose from the bench. "You must excuse me Gentlemen. I have an appointment at five." She turned to Toby. "We will need to sign the share agreement. Do you know the administrative building in New Street. Number twelve, I think."

"I should think I can find it," Toby said.

Can you meet me there at half past the hour of six?"

"Number twelve, New Street at half past six." Toby confirmed.

All present shook hands and parted company.

John and Toby returned to their seats in good spirits. While the turn of events had lifted the two men's spirits, the mood was further enhanced by more good fortune.

No sooner had Elizabeth and her advisor departed, a man approached their table and enquired if they were the masters of a vessel heading for the northern colonies. The man's name was Henk de Groot from the Netherlands. His face did seem vaguely familiar, although that was not unusual in a town of such confined proportions.

It transpired that Mr Groot was seeking passage to the northern colonies and had previously held a position of second-mate with a shipping company operating between Jamaica and Virginia. Should they be interested in taking him on, he could also recommend two other men who were looking for positions as deck-hands.

To Toby, this seemed like a gift from God. However, it appeared John was not willing to take this man on so readily. He insisted on asking questions which seemed to have little relevance to the post: What cargo did the man's previous employer take from Barbados? When loading the sugar, what procedures would he allow for good air circulation? Assuming he was heading north-north-west and had a good wind across the port bow . . . and so on.

It was so unlike the Mate to be so particular. And, to ask such questions of someone who would be hired as a deck-hand seemed completely inappropriate. Such enquiry would be more suitable for the employment of a ship's master. John had to be curtailed.

"Tell me, Mister Groot. How do you occupy your free time?" Toby asked.

The Dutchman considered this for a moment.

"I occupy myself with reading, Captain . . . prose mostly."

Toby raised an eyebrow. "Really?"

"Why, yes. I am reading some English poetry. There is one piece that I am liking very much, but I forget the name." The Dutchman drummed his fingers against his forehead.

The interview was going right off course. Toby had to bring it back.

"It is concerning a tale of –"

"Having held your previous position as second-mate," Toby interrupted. "How would you adjust to the lowly rank of deck hand?"

"That would suit me very well, Captain."

The man had a good command of the English language which, with such a shortage of hands, went in his favour.

"Well, unless Mister Fowler has any more questions, I think we can –"

"With respect, Captain." John gave Toby a sideways look. "Do you not think we should discuss this before coming to any decision?"

Mr Groot excused himself to order a tankard of ale.

Toby leaned across to his Mate and spoke in a hushed tone. "It seems as if fortune is on our side for once, don't you think?"

"I ain't so sure, Captain."

Toby sat up straight. "Why not? Surely you can see we have no option but to take him on!"

"There's something out of sorts with the man. He hardly looks you in the eye. And when he does, it's a cold look if ever there was."

Toby wondered whether his Mate had lost his perspective on practical matters. Had his new position as shareholder in a shipping company gone to his head? It took a good few minutes of discussion before John reluctantly agreed to take the man on.

"Did he not also say he could find us two more hands?" Toby said.

The Mate sighed. "I suppose."

"And was it not you who persuaded me to take on the Burnley man, someone who we know nothing about?"

"Point taken, Captain."

They eventually agreed Henk de Groot should meet them at the dock at six on the following morning providing he could bring along the two extra hands.

After the man had gone, John stood up. "I better see the Mate of that sloop and arrange for the logwood."

Toby also had a number of appointments and time was running by. "So, you'll be back here at eight and let me know the arrangements?"

"Aye, Captain. Here at eight."

Chapter 22 – **Final Night**

Elizabeth was waiting for Toby at the address in New Street. It transpired that arrangements had already been made to have a contract drawn up which was ready to be signed that very afternoon. Magdalena was to remain as manager of La Bruma and, in addition to financial help, Elizabeth would arrange for a land inspector to advise on how to proceed with improvements to the farm. She suggested they should consider this with care as there have been many new arrivals from Suriname of late who are keen to continue their planting habits in Jamaica.

She led Toby outside where their converse could not be overheard. "I envisage there will be some great changes made to the countryside of this island. And sooner than most would expect."

"How will this affect the farm?"

"The Surinamers are planters of sugar cane and they have already taken up much of the available land in the parishes of St Catherine and Clarendon. And considering the difficulties Barbados has been experiencing this past year, it is my belief that this island will soon be a challenging competitor."

Toby was still confused. "Are you suggesting the farm, La Bruma, should consider cultivating the cane?"

"On the contrary, my dear Toby. Considering the size of these new plantations we, La Bruma, would have no chance to compete in the race. What I suggest is that we do the opposite." She paused for a moment as if to give some weight to her words. "While Jamaica, in its hunger for a quick profit, will be taken up with the planting of cane. They will forget all other commodities. And this is where we come in." She studied Toby for a brief moment. "I propose the farm cultivates a product which will have no call for a vast tract of land. A commodity which will also be of value in the colonies where where we are to trade."

"What produce do you have in mind?"

"That will be a matter for our inspector to consider and advise."

Toby wondered how Magdalena would receive all these advances. He mentioned this to Elizabeth.

"I am acquainted with Beatrice's aunt. A formidable lady by all accounts. Methinks we should approach her with caution. Maybe give her some incentive."

Their discourse was interrupted when a clerk stepped out to call them to his office to sign the papers. After the formalities were over Elizabeth again took Toby to one side.

"Do you have any news of Beatrice? I have visited her employer but there appears to be no-one there."

"I did ask Magdalena and she had not heard from her." Toby could see that Elizabeth was concerned. "Unfortunately there is no time for me to call at La Bruma again until I return to Port Royal – we sail at first light tomorrow. Are you acquainted with her aunt well enough to call upon her yourself?"

"As I said before, I am acquainted, but I think she does not approve of me."

Would that deter her? Toby thought not.

"What is it that concerns you? Beatrice seems to be confident in her affairs."

Elizabeth sighed. "She has some information relating to her employer, the knowledge of which could have grave consequences for her. About this, I can say no more."

"I see. Well I promise you, should I have any news of her, I will inform you."

"Thank you, Toby, and I likewise." Elizabeth brightened. "Now, you have my address. Please write and tell me how your first voyage with your new – our new venture transpires."

"I certainly shall. And I will be expecting a letter waiting for me when we reach Virginia. I hope you will have some good news to tell me by then."

"I do too. Well, my dear Toby, let us hope your voyage will be more profitable than the last." She kissed him on the cheek as they parted.

At Fort Charles the desk sergeant informed Toby that an officer had already visited the farm in St Andrews. The occupier had been totally uncooperative and he had not been able to get further than the door. While the sergeant assured him that they would keep a watch on the villa, Toby was not convinced.

After paying the balance for the vessel at the ship handlers, it was nearly eight o'clock when Toby arrived back at the Spar and Halyard. Rather than sit alone in the common room and invite further intrusions, he waited for John in their room. The lamp was topped up with enough oil for several hours light and so Toby set about packing his kitbag. He took out the little box left to him by his father. The letter was missing. He checked inside the bag. Not there either. He must have left it at the farm. However, the content only caused him pain, and he had no need of it now as his interpretation of the code was safe inside the box.

While he waited for John, Toby took up his father's edition of *Lucasta*. The book fell open at a page with a poem entitled *A Loose Saraband with music set by Henry Lawes*: the very words which both Elizabeth and Beatrice were able to sing well on that first night. And now, on his final evening in this town, he was once again in their company, if only in his thoughts.

Beatrice was an enigma. From what Elizabeth had told him, and despite her own accounts, her life seemed to be clouded in mystery. Toby wondered what information she had access to and why it should place her in some sort of danger. Whatever it was, it certainly had Elizabeth concerned. Toby tried to avert his attention to the poem in *Lucasta*.

One hour passed by and still John hadn't shown up. They needed to discuss the arrangements of the logwood consignment. It may well have been that he had forgotten and gone to meet his shipmates. At half past nine there was a knock on the door. It was Davies and Talbert. They were concerned of the whereabouts of the Mate. "We thought he might still be here with you."

"He arranged to meet me here at eight, then to meet you later," said Toby. "I haven't seen him since this afternoon."

"Nor we, Captain."

"This is most unusual." It was not the habit of John to be late for appointments. Toby was now beginning to share their concern. "We sail tomorrow at ten. I think we should look for him."

Starting at the eastern end of High Street, the three men called in at every tavern and drinking house they came to. And there were many. They had almost reached The Old Church when they were met by Matthew Wilkins, arm in arm with two young ladies. He seemed to be self-conscious on meeting them.

"Is John Fowler not with you?" Davies asked.

"No. That's just what I was about to say. A gentleman came up to me and said that he is in trouble, at a place called *Sapatas*. But I don't know where this place is." He made a slight cough. "These two ladies were helping me find the place."

All present seemed to be impressed by Matthew's charming company.

"So that's why we haven't seen much of you since we docked," said Davies.

"Well, hard as it may be Matthew," Toby said. "You best say your farewells to your new friends and report back on board before midnight. We are sailing early in the morning."

They watched Matthew and his two acquaintances head towards New Street. Toby asked Davies if the boy had come to see him about the rope burns the previous morning. Davies confirmed that Matthew did come to see him but the marks were not apparent.

"I know where that *Sapata* place is," said Talbert. "It's near the meat market."

He led the way down a passage which ran parallel to the road where the Merchant's Inn was located. They soon came to a cobbler's with a sign *Sapatas* displayed above the door: the place appeared to be closed. Assuming that Matthew had been given the wrong information, they were about to continue their search when the door was answered. A swarthy gentleman dressed in pantaloons, a tattered undershirt and a pair of leather boots stood behind the crack in the doorway. By his surprised expression the man seemed to be expecting someone else.

"Who is you?" he asked.

"We believe there is a man by the name of Fowler in here," Toby said. "We are from his vessel."

The man opened the door and nodded towards a figure slumped across a table with his head resting in the crook of his arm.

"That he?"

"Yes, that's him." Toby took a step forward.

"Not so fast, Señor." The man held up his hand. They could now see the wide leather baldric slung over the man's shirt held a light cutlass. Two other men appeared at his side, similarly armed. "Unless you pay your friend's bill, he stay here until the militia arrive."

"Well, of course we will settle up. How much is due?"

"Twenty reals."

"Twenty reals!" Davies exclaimed. "No man can drink that worth in one evening!"

"He can. And his amigo."

"What amigo?" asked Toby.

The man glared. "If you not pay, we wait for militia."

"No, no. We'll settle with you," Toby agreed.

Once the money was handed over, the three were let inside. However, this was only the beginning of their troubles: no matter how determined his shipmates were to wake him, John could not be revived. It took all three of them to carry him to the door.

Before they left, Toby again enquired who John's drinking partner happened to be.

"How I know?" the man growled. "You think we ask customers to give name?"

The proprietor had just been paid a vast sum for the release of his customer. Toby was beginning to lose his patience. "There's no need to take that manner –"

"We do apologise for the inconvenience these men have caused you, Sir," said Davies. "I can assure you that they will be dealt with severely. Would you be so good as to give a description of the man who accompanied our friend?"

"I not know. Englishman. Cabelo loiro." The man pointed toward Toby. "Taller than that marinheiro."

Indignant at being classed the same rank as his crew, Toby was about to correct him. Davies stepped between them and again thanked the man for his trouble.

It took all the company to lift John out into the street, and even then they could not revive him. In fact, they decided that their only course of action would be to carry the Mate back to the vessel and hope that he would recover there.

Once they reached the harbour the most difficult task lay ahead. It was with certain trepidation that John's bearers were able to support him up the unstable gangplank. As soon as the party were safely on board the watchman took Toby aside.

"There be somethin' I need bring to your to your attention, Capt'n."

"What is it Jackson?"

"T'were about an hour ago, when I were doin' my rounds, I seen someone slip aboard."

"One of the crew, do you mean?"

"No, Sir. T'were a lad."

"Did you find him?"

"No, Sir. When I first seen him I thinks it were young Matthew."

"Where did he head for, do you think?"

"Scuttled along the gangway up for'ard. Do you want me to go an' look for him, Sir?"

"No, that's all right, Jackson. Let me take care of it. You keep at your station here and let me know if you see anything."

"Aye Sir."

Toby searched the crew's quarters on the forecastle deck and couldn't find anyone there. He also checked the lockers down below and came up with nothing. He could only assume the person had returned ashore, or that Jackson had been spending too much of his takings on rum punch. He returned to the party attending the Mate.

But, no matter how they tried, John didn't come round. Even after emptying a pail of water over the man's head, John did not so much as stir. They laid him out in the captain's bunk and, fearing the man was likely to have been drugged, they considered whether to call for the aid of a physician. However, it was now just before midnight and it would be difficult to find anyone at this hour.

Matthew turned up just before twelve and the four of them sat out on the main deck of the Dunstan. The Mate's mysterious drinking partner now became their topic of conversation. They considered the description they had been given by the proprietor at the cobbler's – a tall Englishman.

Talbert also remembered the proprietor saying something else. Something in Spanish.

"Portuguese," corrected Davies. "He said the other man was *Cabelo loiro*. He had light-brown hair."

Tallish with light-brown hair: hardly conclusive, thought Toby. "What about the man who warned of John's whereabouts?"

Matthew tried to remember. A frail pasty-faced man with a long dark wig. This didn't match the other man's description at all. They could only wait for John to come round before getting the answer. The four decided to stay on board overnight and collect their victuals from their lodgings the following morning. Toby took a hammock on the poop deck.

At a little after five Toby was awoken by the watchman.

"Captain, there be a lighter alongside!"

Toby strained his eyes in the darkness.

"What?"

Fearing robbers were attempting to board the vessel in the dead of night, Toby ordered him to arouse the others.

Toby, pistol at the ready, was soon joined by Davies and Matthew Wilkins. All three leaned over the port gunwale to face a group of four suspicious gentlemen standing in a barge looking back up to them.

"Who's there?" Toby called.

"We're to speak to Mister Fowler," a brusque voice answered.

"What business do you want with him?"

"Who be you to ask?"

"The master."

The man turned to speak to his colleagues then looked back up to Toby. "Fair enough, we have your consignment here, as arranged."

Toby stared into the hold of the lighter – the logwood. Of course! What with all the recent events, he had forgotten about the cargo his Mate had arranged.

"How much is there?"

"Fifteen tons."

"How much did John. . . Mister Fowler pay you?"

"Pay us? Listen here, your Mister Fowler ain't paid us nought! If you is trying to play games with us, we'll scupper this tub of yours in next to no time! The agreement was one hundred an' eighty pounds, and you better have it or I'll have you lot quartered!" The man looked like he meant every word.

Toby looked at the others alongside him at the rail. "Is John up yet?"

All shook their heads. Toby leaned back over the side.

"Hold on for two minutes."

"Any longer and we're off skipper. And you're sunk!"

Toby hurried to his cabin. He had to know if John had exchanged any money with these sea robbers. But the Mate was still flat out on his back: the same position as they left him six hours before. Nothing would rouse him.

Toby did a few calculations on his way back to the deck. Fifteen tons of logwood would hopefully fetch three hundred pounds up in Boston with Messrs Faber and Wilks. He leant over the rail and called down to the men in the barge. "Eighty pounds."

"You're asking to lose an ear, Skipper!" The man had his hand resting on the hilt of his cutlass. "And we'll pop a few grenades through your window for the bargain."

Toby turned to the others, who were looking a little paled in the first light of day.

"Do you reckon we could take them on?"

"Captain," Davies began, always ready to offer a reply. "With respect, I believe this consignment probably comes from that sloop over there."

Toby looked across the harbour to the twin-masted vessel moored out in the middle of the bay; a fair sized sloop mounted with over a dozen canon – of course Davies was right, he always was. Toby leaned back over the rail. "One hundred. That's my final offer."

"One-fifty. That's my last warning!"

"Done."

"Send it over then, skipper."

"Only if one of you stays on board here. You'll get half now and the rest when it's all loaded."

"Fair enough. But you'll have to send one of your men down with it. The fair-haired lad."

Toby reluctantly sent Matthew over with half of the payment while a seaman, his body covered in tattoos, stepped aboard the Dunstan.

The logs, stripped and cut into five foot lengths, were loaded at the bottom of the hold. It was necessary that they be stowed away out of sight and covered with canvas to avoid detection by the customs. With the shortage of available hands, it took over an hour and a half to load and it was daylight by the time they had finished.

It was agreed that the crew would muster aboard at seven that morning. Samuel Taponket, the bosun, was always reliable and reported to Toby at the appointed time. Samuel was not the sort of man who gave away much of his personal life, in fact there were few who could tell you his original name. It was a mystery how this giant of a man amused himself in his free time, for no matter where they docked, as soon as he stepped ashore he just disappeared.

They were due a cargo of sixteen tons of sugar which would be loaded from the quayside and Toby asked Samuel to make sure this was stowed to cover the logwood in the hold. It was whilst they were discussing this matter that the new hand, Burnley, came on board. It was later that morning that at least two of the crew commented that his features fitted the description of the man seen drinking with their Mate the evening before. Toby made a note to ask John about the event and see if he had any recollection of it being this man. He took the opportunity to take a look at the Mate before the cargo arrived. John had turned onto his side in the bunk but still nothing could wake him.

When Toby returned on deck, he came face to face with three new hands. The Dutchman, Henk de Groot, was accompanied by the two recruits he had promised to bring with him. The first was short, stocky, had an untidy beard and head of dark hair, while the other was slim, clean shaven and stood about six feet tall – the three could not have looked less alike. There was no time to interview them as the sugar consignment had arrived at the quayside and Toby was required to arrange the loading. He asked the three men to report to the bosun who would find them plenty enough to do.

"Not the Mate, Captain?" asked Groot.

"No, the bosun. He's the Indian. You can't miss him. Stands well above the others."

"I'm sure we'll find him, Captain."

The three headed off to the main deck. Neither of the recruits who accompanied Groot had said a word to Toby.

The sugar arrived on time, wheeled along the narrow jetty in hand-carts pulled by over twenty Negro slaves. The loading of this cargo was operated so efficiently that, by one hour past noon, the Dunstan was heading out into the crystal blue waters of the Caribbean.

Chapter 23 – **Passage to Nevis**

On leaving Port Royal the Dunstan made a disappointing four knots. However, watching the houses on that peninsula disappear over the horizon was no loss to Toby. To feel the fresh breeze on his cheek and breathe in the salt air was a sensation he had longed for over the past two weeks. Keeping the prevailing north-easterly three points on the port bow, the Dunstan picked up speed and maintained a steady course throughout the next two days. Although Toby was happy to leave Port Royal his thoughts were on the villa in St Andrews and those he had left behind.

"You wanted to see me, Captain?" Groot had turned up on the poop.

"Ah yes, Mister Groot. I wonder if you could help me?"

"Yes, Captain?" The Dutchman was standing with his arms to his side in a respectful stance.

"The two hands, Mitchell and Orleans. They seem to be a little out of sorts with commonplace routines on board. Do you know if they have been to sea before?"

"That's what they have told me, Captain."

"Is that so?"

"Yes, Sir. But I do agree with you, Captain, I have been noticing they have few seamanship skills."

"If any," Toby added.

"May I make a suggestion, Captain?"

"Go ahead."

"Would it be of use to you if I should be taking these two men in hand and to training them?"

"It would seem to be our only option, Mister Groot. Yes, I would appreciate that."

The man turned to go, then hesitated.

"Is there something else?"

"Well, yes Captain. I notice we are keeping an easterly setting. We are not heading for the Windward Passage?"

"Very observant of you, Mister Groot." Toby studied the Dutchman. "I have been warned that there have been many attacks on merchant vessels by the Spanish of late," he lied. "For all our safety, I have decided to keep clear of these islands and head north for Virginia once we pass Saint Domingue." Toby scratched his chin. "Oh, yes. I would appreciate it if you could relay this to the crew when you return."

The Dutchman considered this for a moment, but said nothing.

"That'll be all, Mister Groot?"

"Oh, yes Sir. Thank you, Captain."

Toby watched the Dutchman steady himself at the rail as he returned to the main deck. The man seemed confident with his duties but had yet to find his sea legs. However, over the next few days Mr Groot would prove to be a useful aide, particularly with regard to the two hands in his charge.

Burnley, however, was another matter. It had been brought to his notice on several occasions that he fitted the description given by the proprietor of the grog shop in Port Royal. For this reason Toby felt a little uneasy about having him on board. When Davies came up to take over the watch that evening, Toby asked for his opinion of the new hand.

"He seems to be fine, Sir. Although, he doesn't say much."

"Does he behave in a suspicious manner in any way?"

"No, Sir. Just keeps to himself."

Toby was convinced Davies hadn't noticed the man at all since he came on board. He decided to let the subject go. "Have you attended the Mate this afternoon?"

"Yes Sir, only just now I called in on him. He's still very drowsy. I gave him some quinine, but it didn't seem to have any effect. I believe he should get some air, now the sun is down."

Davies always had an answer to everything, thought Toby. "Very well, I'll see if he's up to it when I come off watch." Toby handed over the log and gave him the setting.

"With respect, Sir. Are we not heading for the Dominica passage?"

Toby was puzzled. "Did not Mister Groot tell you? We are heading for the Virgin Isles."

"No, Sir. The Dutchman does not talk to any of the crew. Apart from his two shipmates, that is."

"Much like the man Burnley?"

"No, Captain, not like Burnley at all. Groot, only talks to Mitchell and the Frenchman. He has no time for the rest of us. In fact, he –"

"Yes, I've asked him to take them in his charge. I find Mister Groot a very helpful aid to the running of this vessel. In fact, I have decided that, until the Mate is well enough to resume his duties, I am appointing Mister Groot to stand in for him."

There was a pause before Davies spoke. "Do you think that wise, Sir?"

"Yes, I do."

While Davies had been a loyal member of Toby's crew from the very beginning, there had always been a little friction between him and his captain. Toby somehow felt the man held some grudge against him. It could be that Davies was resentful at not being offered a promotion during his service or maybe it was just that he could sense Toby's disapproval of his comradeship with John Fowler. Whatever the reason, the matter had never actually come to a head.

"There is another thing, Captain."

Toby sighed. "Go on, Mister Davies."

"A dispute has developed amongst some of the crew."

"What kind of dispute?"

"Some of the hands have had their food rations taken."

"By Mister Groot, I presume?"

"No, Sir. Not Mister Groot. At least we don't know that."

"But you assume it?"

Davies didn't comment. "It's just that on a number of occasions, whenever any victuals have been left unattended, the items have mysteriously vanished. The plate has been left clean. As if we have a hungry dog aboard."

"Did you not check there were enough provisions to go around when we left Port Royal?"

"That's just it, Sir. There are no shortage of rations. It's as if someone is trying to start a conflict between the crew."

"I advise you to keep a close watch on that man Burnley."

"Yes Sir, but I really don't think –"

"Well, that's settled," said Toby. "Mister Groot will take over from you at the next watch."

"Aye, Captain."

Toby left the poop deck and went down below to his quarters.

While John Fowler was able to prop himself up on one elbow for a few seconds, that was the extent of his improvement, no doubt waylaid by the dose of quinine. His conversation was limited to a nonsensical babbling and even this seemed to drain all his energy.

There was little improvement in the Mate's health over the next two days and it wasn't until the fourth day of the voyage that John was well enough to take a few steps out on deck. After this, he made a miraculous recovery. On the following morning, after a breakfast of fish kedgeree and rice, John was well enough to take the first watch. Toby broached the subject of his last night in Port Royal.

"Can you recall anything of that evening?"

John Fowler ran his hand over his whiskers. "The last thing I remember was returning from the meeting with Captain O'Malley."

"O'Malley?"

"The skipper of that sloop from Campechy."

"Oh yes. That reminds me. You didn't give them a deposit did you?"

"No, certainly not, Captain!"

"Fine, that's good. How much did you settle for?"

"One hundred pounds for eighteen tonnes."

"Eighteen? They only brought fifteen."

"How much did you pay them for that, Captain?"

"One-fifty."

"One hundred and fifty pounds! You must be . . . I'm sorry Captain, but I reckon we've been had."

Toby folded his arms. "Yes, but we'll get twice that for it when we get to Boston."

John steadied himself against the rail and shook his head. "I'm not sure I can afford that much," he muttered.

"Look, John. Don't concern yourself. If you prefer, we can alter our arrangement." Toby wanted to steer the conversation back to his Mate's drinking companion. "When you left O'Malley, did you meet up with anyone else? If you remember we had arranged to see each other at eight that evening,"

John was silent for a few moments. "No, Captain. I can't remember meeting anyone." He shook his head. "One-fifty for fifteen tonnes," he muttered.

From then on John made good recovery and by the following day he was able to return to his duties as Mate of the Dunstan.

Over the next few days the vessel made steady progress and the passage was uneventful. Mr Groot had been working closely with the two hands in his charge and there was much improvement in their abilities. While their reluctance to go aloft remained a challenge, simple tasks such as stowing away lines and repairing canvas were mastered satisfactorily. It would only be a matter of time before they would find their way. The other new recruit, Burnley, turned out to be a very capable seaman and had settled well with the remaining crew. However, Toby's opinion of the man remained somewhat reserved. He asked the Mate if there had been further disputes concerning food rations.

"Not disputes exactly, Captain. More confusions."

"Confusions?"

"The men are of the opinion there may be rats aboard. They have set a few traps around their quarters but, as of yet, none of the bait has been taken."

"And the food rations?"

"Well that's just it. The odd meal still goes missing."

"Has anyone attempted to keep a watch down there?"

"Being that we are very short of hands, there's no-one that can be spared, Sir."

Toby still had reservations about Burnley.

"Well, whenever you have a moment, Mister Fowler, perchance you could take a look for yourself," he suggested. "After all, we don't want this to cause resentment between the crew, and particularly if there is a someone who is causing this conundrum."

"Yes Sir." John hesitated. "Mister Davies did say you had your suspicions."

"Ah yes. Well, I'm in no doubt that he did. No doubt at all, Mister Fowler."

Chapter 24 – A Peculiar Request

At eight in the evening on Wednesday 23nd of October, Toby arrived on deck to relieve the Mate.

"What's our estimated arrival time for Nevis, Mister Fowler?"

"Seven forenoon, Captain."

"Could you send word to the crew that we shall be calling there to take on fresh water."

"Aye, but considering the small number on board, would it not be best if it came from you?"

"Why would that be, Mister Fowler?"

"Oh, just an idea, Captain." John refused to rise to the challenge. "I'll set to it right away."

Toby watched the Mate make his way to the main deck. Why is it that even the most simple commands have to be questioned? He turned to the man at the tiller. "What's the heading, Mister Jackson?"

"East by south-east, Sir."

With a prevailing south-westerly, the Dunstan made good headway during the night and by 4.30 the following morning the Isle of Nevis was sighted on the horizon. When viewing the chart, the island gave the appearance of a ball which had been tossed to the south by its nearest neighbour, St Christopher. The island measured little more than five miles across with Charles Town keeping watch over the Western Caribbean. By daybreak the vessel was half a league from the port awaiting permission to dock.

The Captain and John Fowler were both standing at the starboard rail; a clear morning air giving them a good view of the town and western approaches. Like many in the region, the island was once a raging volcano which had forced its way to the surface of the ocean. Now quietened, the mountain was obscured by cloud which gave the impression it was covered in snow.

"Looks like sugar fever has taken over this place too, eh Captain?"

From the edge of the shore, up to the slopes of the mountain, every available acre of arable land was taken up with the planting of cane.

"And the importation of Negroes to harvest it, it seems" said Toby.

It was difficult to estimate the number of dark-skinned field workers on the hillside, but the tally must have run into the many hundreds.

Toby nodded towards a lonely chapel north of the town and set back from the coast. "And I believe that could be our place, John."

Within an hour of docking the Captain and Mate of the Dunstan stepped ashore and made their way up the hill to make an inspection of the chapel.

The Church of Saint Thomas stood on an area of cleared land at the end of a long rough track two miles north of Charles Town. The cemetery was positioned on high ground giving the visitor a spectacular view of the neighbouring island of Saint Christopher. Toby tried to imagine what his father had been doing here. Going by past experience, there would be little point enquiring at the militia office and, under present circumstances, it wouldn't be wise to draw attention to themselves.

There were many graves to examine, most belonging to the casualties of the conflicts with the French over the past few decades. Each headstone was simply inscribed with a name and a date and many with the date 1667. Most were men of a similar age so there must have been some tragic military event on the island in that year.

"Over here, Captain. I think I've found one of them." John was standing at the last row, nearest to the track. The headstone was inscribed John Mortimer and the dates 1642-1668. Another grave, just six feet away was marked Daniel Keach 1645-1668.

Toby and John looked at each other in amazement. They had both taken a chance based on a supposition: the addendum to the letter from Toby's father could have been a mere ruse to divert those who were out to steal his fortune, and the reference to the song may have been a sentimental remembrance of a childhood diversion. They now faced the possibility that the suggestion in the letter could be a truth. However, so taken up were they with the chase, the two adventurers had not looked beyond this. They now had to consider their next move.

The location of the cemetery presented a few problems; while the road was obscured from the fields on each side by dense vegetation, a journey laden with two large boxes would be arduous, if not impossible. Also the graveyard was exposed to the south; any activity could easily be observed by the people in the town.

With heavy hearts they made their way back down the deserted track.

"What if we had some help?" John suggested.

"How could we, without disclosing our business?"

They continued in silence, each with their own thoughts, until they reached the town. At the little Town Square, Toby came to a halt. He studied the administrative building across the way. "I have an idea."

Back at the ship John Fowler sat at the desk in his captain's quarters. Two documents, written on the best quality parchment, were laid out before him. The first was an original letter of recommendation from the Governor's Office of Virginia requesting that a shipment of arms be transported from Barbados to Virginia. Although he couldn't understand the meaning behind many of the words on the page, John was bent over the second document for the good part of half of an hour. Every stroke of the quill was copied with undivided concentration; every detail reproduced with utmost care. The copy was identical to the original. There were, however, a few alterations; the date was put back by seven weeks, the document was addressed to the Governor of Nevis, and the request was no longer for a shipment of armaments, but for the exhumation of the bodies of two ex-servicemen to be transported back to their homes in Virginia.

John waited for the signature to dry then passed both documents to his captain. "What do you think? Will this pass?"

Toby studied the papers for a few minutes, then looked up. "Excellent."

"There is only one problem that I can see, Captain."

"And what would that be?"

"Ain't it custom for these papers to be sealed?"

"Indeed so, and that's where another of your skills come into play."

Toby took the original document and folded the page, neatly bringing together the break in the seal.

"I would like you to make an impression of this design, and from it fashion a new seal. Can you do that?"

For the next thirty minutes John worked his sculpting knife at the face of a small block; pealing away minuscule slithers of the wood, holding his example up to the light to compare with the original, continually making further adjustments until at last the work was complete.

Toby dropped some melted wax on a fresh page and pressed the seal into it. They both leaned forward to inspect.

Toby screwed his eyes as he moved from one seal to the other. "I see no difference."

The Mate sat back and stretched his arms. "She'll do, I guess."

The office of the Governor's Secretary was on the upper floor of the Administrative building in Charles Town. Toby was asked to wait in a long corridor decorated with paintings which depicted scenes of the French ports. There was an official notice fixed to the door;

As a gesture of good will and with the intent of prolonging recent peace between our two islands, this office and the corresponding Office of Governor of Saint Christophers have come to the mutual agreement to exchange secretaries for the duration of one year. Mr James Markham will be taking up duties in Basseterre and I hope all will welcome the presence of Monsieur Jules Plumepince at this office without prejudice. Philip James Langley Gov. Nevis April 1675.

That's all I need, thought Toby; a French official! The paintings should have warned him.

It was at least twenty minutes before the clerk appeared and showed him into a large room with a window overlooking the town square. Monsieur Plumepince, who continued to busy himself at his desk, had an unhealthy complexion and wore an extravagant grey wig which did nothing but exaggerate his pinched features.

Without looking up, the man indicated the chair opposite his sumptuous desk.

"'ow may I 'elp you, Monsieur?

"I have a letter from the Governor's Office of Virginia which is for your attention."

This did little to impress. The official let out a sigh and held out an extended hand. He took the document over to the window and broke the seal without a second glance.

Toby sat at the desk, hardly daring to breathe.

Eventually, the man folded the letter and studied Toby with a serious expression. "This is an unusual request, Monsieur Opkin." He waved the document. "You are aware of the procedures?" He moved forward and lifted a heavy brass bell from his desk.

The ringing continued in Toby's ears long after it had been replaced. "Well, yes. I think I –"

There was a knock and the man who had first shown Toby into the room, entered and stood by the door. "Oui, Monsieur?"

Monsieur Plumepince spoke a few words in French. The man left, only to return a few moments later bearing a file. Toby did his best to stay calm. He shifted his weight in the chair as the official ran his finger down the list of names.

"Mortimer and Quiche, you say?" Monsieur Plumepince looked up from the file.

Toby had to think quickly. "I have not been given the details of this assignment, Sir."

"Ah, I see." He placed the file on his desk and went on to explain every detail of the task, emphasising to Toby the importance of his assignment. "Do you 'ave a cold store room on your sheep?"

"Yes, we do," Toby lied.

"And what are the contents of this?"

There was a knock on the door and a pasty-faced clerk wearing an extravagant periwig staggered in.

"Ah yes, Monsieur Butcher. This is Mister Opkin, he is master of the Merchant Vessel, er . . ." he looked toward Toby.

"The Dunstan," Toby prompted.

"Oui, le Doonstan." Monsieur Plumepince cleared his throat. "I 'ave been asked that two bodies are to be taken from the cemetery of Saint Thomas and loaded aboard 'is vessel." He turned to Toby. "Of course, this is a very unusual request and would normally take many days to prepare." He raised a brow. "Do you 'ave a liste des cargaisons?"

Toby frowned.

The official looked towards the man swaying near the door.

"I think what Monsieur Plumepince is saying," the clerk pulled the ringlets from his eyes. "Is that he is wondering if there is anything in your vessel that could be of interest to him, if you get my drift, Captain?"

"Oh, I see. Well, we have a consignment of rum –"

"Alors! C'est pour les Anglais!" the official gave Toby a look of disapproval.

"Sugar?" Toby ventured.

The clerk intervened. "Have you not noticed, Captain, how the island has been taken over with new plantations?"

"But is good for to sweeten le chocolate," the official added.

"Chocolate is all the fashion in France, so I believe," continued the clerk. "They drink the stuff until it comes out of their . . . " His words tailed off and he glanced towards the Frenchman.

"We do have a small consignment of cocoa," Toby suggested.

"Oui?" Monsieur Plumepince's expression brightened.

"I'm sure one sack would not go amiss."

The man shrugged. "Only one?" He pursed his lips.

"Two sacks then," Toby said. "I'll have them brought up here this afternoon.

"Bon!" Monsieur Plumepince turned to the clerk who was having difficulty steadying himself against the door frame. "I would like you to arrange that an 'orse and carriage and two grave diggers be placed at Monsieur Opkin's disposal."

"Yes Sir, when will you require this, Sir?"

The official looked towards Toby with eyebrows raised.

"We plan to sail on the afternoon tide tomorrow," Toby said.

"Can that be arranged, Monsieur Butcher?"

"That'll be fine, Sir." The clerk turned to Toby. "Shall we say at the square here at ten, Captain?"

"Yes, thank you." Toby watched the man stagger through the door, convinced he'd met him before.

Back aboard *The Dunstan*, John could hardly believe their luck when he was told the news.

"So, if we are both to rendez-vous with the clerk tomorrow, we will need someone to watch the loading of the water which is due to arrive soon after daybreak."

"I'll ask Bosun to do that, shall I?" John paused. "Or, shall I ask Mister Davies?"

Toby gave the Mate a look. "The Bosun will do, thank you Mister Fowler."

The carriage ride to St Thomas Church was bumpy to say the least. The two passengers gripped the sides of the wagon as it rocked its way up the hill. They looked to each other with the same thought; would the boxes, deteriorated after years beneath the earth, be able to withstand the journey?

The dig went without incident apart from one dreadful moment. Just as the second box was lifted from the grave, the rope gave way. The coffin crashed to the clay with a solid thud. Toby had a vision of the contents spilling over the floor of the grave for all to see. But it held fast and was soon loaded onto the cart alongside its neighbour.

At 13.00, the boxes were the last of the cargo to be brought aboard. They were stowed away into a secure forecastle locker just forward of the main deck. The only access to this locker was through a door which could be observed at any time from the poop.

With three hours before sailing, Toby and John entered the locker room. Like children waiting for the grand opening of the fair, they stood before the crates with no certainty of what lay on the other side of the dark stained wood. What if they had misinterpreted the message and the boxes really *did* contain military personnel whose only failing was to serve God and Country? The two entrepreneurs stood before the first box, one holding up an oil lamp, the other gripping an iron bar.

"Ready, John?"

"Aye, let's get to it, Captain."

At the first heave, the lid came away without a sound and slid gently off to the side. With his hand poised at the corner of the canvas lining, Toby made a grimace. What a relief it was to discover four jute sacks resting at the base of the crate. They pulled out the first.

Toby pressed the point of his knife into the sacking. His heart sank. A gentle stream of soft sand issued from the cut. He put his fingers into the split and ripped it open. The sack spilled its entire contents onto the deck. They were surrounded by sand; nothing more, nothing less, just grey volcanic grit. John bent forward and sank his fingers into the bag at his end of the box. There was a resistance, something solid. Both men straightened up. For a moment they both stared at the sack, each not daring to be the first to venture further.

John tapped the bag gently with his iron: this time a clunk, the sound of metal against metal.

Almost simultaneously, the two men dived at the remaining sacks. Like wild hunting dogs they ripped at the canvas with their knives, splitting the bags open until every item spilled out onto the deck. Toby grabbed the lamp and held it high. Gold coins were scattered at their feet, richly coloured stones of various hues, silver chalices, gold figures, all glinting in the lamplight.

They moved over to the second coffin and yanked its lid off without hesitation. As if the contents of the first casket were not sufficient enough, the second held even more. Not two, but three sacks displayed their contents to the two men: booty enough to set them up for life.

Both Toby and John stood still for a very long time, each not daring to disturb the silence should the spell be broken.

John was the first to speak. "Well, what now?"

Toby ran his finger across his chin. "I think it best that we put it all back in the cases and keep them here. The safest place. Do you agree, John?"

They collected every item from the floor until the sacks were refilled. The lids of the boxes secured, both men stepped out onto the deck and locked the door behind them.

"Is there only one key to this locker, John?"

"No Sir, there is another hanging in the store room."

Toby cast an eye about. The only figures in sight were battening down the main hatch; Samuel the boatswain and one of the new hands, Jack.

"We should each hold a key and not let it leave our person."

"I'll fetch the other right now."

"Good. Meet me in my quarters when you finish your watch. We need to think this through."

"Aye, Captain."

It was difficult to estimate the value of such a large haul. Their next task, if it could be called such, was how and where they should exchange the bounty for ready money. John had come to join the captain in his cabin below the after-deck. He held up the locker key and placed it in his pocket. "I reckon we'd be best to wait till we get to Boston." suggested John.

"Do you not think James Town?"

"We have no contacts in Virginia." John drew on his pipe and sent up a cloud of blue smoke. "We could be taken for a couple of sprats in a pot."

Toby got up from his desk and opened the window behind the Mate's chair. "Fair point, John. Boston it is. Have you any thoughts on who we can take it to?"

There's a jewellers in East Street. Benjamin Schenker. I've done some business with him afore. Gives a fair deal."

Toby raised an eyebrow. He was about to ask the nature of the Mate's business, but thought the better of it. "We had better take account of all we have, then devise a strategy before we let anyone know of our prize. What do you say, John?"

"Sounds fine to me, Captain."

John got up from his chair. "Those three new hands were down in the hold on cargo watch today. Best I go and check everything is stowed away properly. What time are we due to sail, Captain?"

"At half-past the hour of four." Toby glanced at the chronometer above his desk. "Just over an hour."

Left to his own thoughts, Toby reflected on how this haul could change everything; a new vessel, new trading ventures, improvements to La Bruma. At last the tide had turned. These thoughts of optimism only lasted a few moments before the familiar self-doubts returned. Could this turn for good fortune be lasting? Only time will tell.

END

About the Author

James Faro joined the Merchant Navy at the age of sixteen, travelling extensively throughout Brazil, North America and the Caribbean. He has lived in many countries including Spain, Portugal, Cyprus, Aden and the Netherlands. Now living in Brighton, England, he has retained his fascination with travel and the sea which is reflected in his writing.

See glossary of terms used in this book at
www.jamesfaro.com

Printed in Great Britain
by Amazon

66926351R00149